Denver flicked a finger at the window that looked out over the beach.

"Is someone giving you a heads-up about this case? How do you know it's not the killer of that girl in the trunk? How do you know he's not just toying with you? Hoping for some publicity?"

The skin around Ashlynn's luscious mouth turned white. Her blue eyes watered, and she dabbed her nose with a napkin.

"Who said anyone is contacting me about the case? I literally stumbled over a car in Lake Kawayu and then came out to Venice for a walk. Someone decided to conk me on the head and mug me."

He narrowed his eyes. "That's the way you want to play it? Clicks or whatever you're after are more important than finding the killer of this girl?"

She swirled her drink. "I don't have anything to give you, Detective—no evidence, no clues. I can't solve this case for you."

"You got that right." He smacked his hand on the table, rattling the glasses. "So don't even try."

LAKESIDE MYSTERY

——

CAROL ERICSON

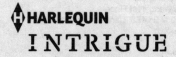

HARLEQUIN®
INTRIGUE™

ISBN-13: 978-1-335-58207-2

Lakeside Mystery

Copyright © 2022 by Carol Ericson

Harlequin Enterprises ULC
22 Adelaide St. West, 41st Floor
Toronto, Ontario M5H 4E3, Canada
www.Harlequin.com

Printed in U.S.A.

Carol Ericson is a bestselling, award-winning author of more than forty books. She has an eerie fascination for true crime stories, a love of film noir and a weakness for reality TV, all of which fuel her imagination to create her own tales of murder, mayhem and mystery. To find out more about Carol and her current projects, please visit her website at www.carolericson.com, "where romance flirts with danger."

Books by Carol Ericson

Harlequin Intrigue

The Lost Girls

Canyon Crime Scene
Lakeside Mystery

A Kyra and Jake Investigation

The Setup
The Decoy
The Bait
The Trap

Holding the Line

Evasive Action
Chain of Custody
Unraveling Jane Doe
Buried Secrets

Visit the Author Profile page at Harlequin.com.

CAST OF CHARACTERS

Denver Holt—This LAPD detective will do almost anything to get on the homicide squad, even if it means cooperating with a meddling blogger with questionable motives.

Ashlynn Hughes—She took over her murdered brother's true crime blog and now has the opportunity of a lifetime to prove herself her brother's equal...if it weren't for the sexy detective cramping her style.

Tiana Fields—A political volunteer, she winds up dead in the trunk of a car, and her murder sends shock waves through the LA mayoral race.

Angel—An anonymous tipster to Ashlynn's blog, he claims to know Tiana's secrets...secrets that just might get him killed.

Veronica Escalante—This savvy politician is challenging the mayor and will do anything to replace him.

Kent Meadows—Veronica's wealthy husband is happy to fund his wife's campaign, as long as she doesn't snoop into his extracurricular activities.

Mayor Wexler—The mayor of LA is up for reelection, and the last thing he needs is a whiff of scandal and a blogger with inside information.

Chapter One

A shiver snaked through Ashlynn's body, even though the sun streamed through the branches of the trees, creating a dappled pattern on the ground. She hugged herself, clutching her pepper spray in one hand against her upper arm. Her brother, Sean, had agreed to meet someone near a lake…and it hadn't ended well for him.

Of course, she wasn't exactly meeting someone, and Sean had traipsed out in the dead of night. Unlike her foolish brother, she'd ventured out in the middle of the day with hikers panting along the trail and mountain bikers kicking up dirt as they trundled up the hill. Her nose tingled with tears and she wiped her sleeve across it. Nobody could tell Sean anything.

He had been a successful true crime blogger because he'd embraced danger, taken those necessary risks. She'd have to remold herself in his image if she hoped to keep his blog going strong. She didn't want *LA Confidential* to die with her brother.

She puffed out her cheeks and trudged onward. She'd venture as far as the lake, have a look around, maybe take a few pictures, and wait for the next message—if there was a next message. If her anonymous contact didn't send her another communication after the first one about a submerged car in Lake Kawayu, she'd look for another story to feature on the blog.

Stopping under a tree, she tapped her phone to bring up the trail map and had to lunge out of the way of oncoming runners. She called into their dust. "Where's the turnoff for the lake?"

One of them yelled something unintelligible but pointed to his right. Another several yards and Ashlynn spotted the weathered sign pointing toward Lake Kawayu. How could a car possibly make its way down a trail like this to plunge into a lake?

She veered to the right between two oaks, their leaves dripping water from the rain the day before.

Ashlynn shuffled downhill through the debris of leaves, twigs and pebbles that littered the trail. Any minute she expected to see the lake through the branches of the trees, but spring had done its job and the forest bloomed and flourished around her so that she could barely see beyond the next bend.

When the foliage thinned, and a couple toting a fiberglass canoe squeezed past her, she knew she was close.

She rounded the next corner and caught her breath as a dark blue ripple appeared below. She had to scrabble down a small incline to reach the shore of the lake, and she placed her hands on her hips and took a deep breath of the pine and earthy muddy scent that assailed her.

She scanned the perimeter of the body of water, her gaze lingering on the north shore where a dirt parking lot boasted several cars belonging to people who knew they didn't need to hike a mile and a half to reach the lake. She also realized that if a car were going to plunge into the water, that parking lot had to be its origination point.

Shading her eyes, she judged the distance to the parking lot to be another half mile. She glanced at the sturdy sneakers on her feet and pulled a bottle of water from her small daypack. She took a long gulp of water and watched the couple launch their canoe into the lake with a splash. She'd come prepared— and she needed a new story for the blog.

Her shoes crunched the coarse sand lakeside as she started walking the semicircle to the parking lot. She didn't know why her anonymous tipster had contacted her—probably because *LA Confidential* still sported the sheen of her brother's success— but she didn't want to dismiss it. Sean had told her some of his best stories started as anonymous bits of information.

If this were just a submerged car, she'd blow it off, but the tipster had claimed there was a dead body in the car. The least she could do was check it out. It's not like she had a lot on her plate. She'd quit her job at the magazine when Sean was…killed. She couldn't go back to it now, and she didn't want to. Sean had died just when his blog had hit peak popularity, and she felt an obligation to carry on with it. She'd had a modicum of success with her first story—an exposé of Reed Dufrain, addiction recovery guru turned drug dealer—but she couldn't rest on her laurels.

A few families frolicked in the water, and Ashlynn shivered. Must be out-of-towners, because it was definitely too cold for thin-blooded Angelenos to take a dip. Summer was still a season away, and the sun starting to make its appearance every day lacked the wattage of an August or September in LA.

Still, Ashlynn had a one-piece on under her clothes and a towel rolled up in her pack. How else could she spot a submerged car? Maybe one of these swimmers would discover it first and save her the trouble of a chilly dip.

When she reached the parking lot, she downed more water from her bottle. She nodded at a group stoking the flames in a hibachi, paper plates of bratwurst and burgers standing by. She was pretty sure the city didn't allow an open fire like that in Angeles Crest, but she wasn't here to be Smokey the Bear's helper.

She wandered to the edge of the dirt lot, facing the water. No barrier or lip separated the lot from the lakeshore, and plenty of tire tracks indicated that people drove right up to the water's edge. Into the water?

She scuffed through the sand and rocks up to the dark, oily water lapping the banks. No swimmers had ventured into the lake from the parking area. They most likely preferred the cleaner-looking water down from the trees, but that probably explained why nobody had found the car yet.

Sighing, Ashlynn swung the pack off her back and dropped it in the dirt. She fished out her towel, shook it and set it next to her daypack. Then she toed off her shoes and wriggled free of her clothes, quickly, kicking both onto the towel.

She waded into the water, her arms folded over her chest, goose bumps crawling across her bare flesh. When the water reached her hips, she pushed off the rocky bottom with her feet and paddled into the murky lake. The parking lot wasn't that wide and a car launched from the banks couldn't go that far. She did a breaststroke in a line horizontal to the shore, kicking her legs in a wide circle and peering into the water. She moved a little farther into the water and repeated her course back the other way.

A few people from the barbecuing bunch in the parking lot stood at its edge, staring at her. She supposed she must look a little crazy to people watching, but as she took another stroke, she muttered, "I'll never see them again."

The lake had gotten deep fast, and her toes no longer even skimmed the bottom. A whole car could definitely be submerged under the water and nobody would notice it from the shore.

As she circled into another wide turn, her fluttering feet made contact with something hard and smooth…and big. Holding her breath, she ducked beneath the water and opened her eyes. She flipped and swam downward for a few feet. Her hands met solid metal before she saw its glint.

Her lungs bursting, she propelled herself to the

surface and gasped in a long breath. She'd found the car. Was there a body inside?

DETECTIVE DENVER HOLT stared over his clenched hands on the steering wheel at a knot of people gathered at the edge of the murky lake. The hoist to lift the car from the cloudy depths was already in place, and he could imagine the divers below hooking up the winches. His captain had sent him on another thrilling adventure to assist the traffic division with an accident or possible stolen while his name languished on the list for Robbery-Homicide.

He smacked the steering wheel with the heels of his hands. He'd sworn to protect and serve—even victims of auto theft. He exited his sedan and strode toward the commotion, his wing tips crunching the sand and gravel on the shore of the lake.

"Detective Holt." Flashing his badge at the uniform, he asked, "Have the divers indicated yet if there's anyone in the car?"

"Officer Brooks." Brooks tapped his nametag and shrugged. "If they found anything, they haven't told me about it. I'm here for crowd control."

Denver scanned the smattering of people and smirked. Some crowd. "Who discovered the car?"

Brooks jerked his thumb over his shoulder. "The woman with the towel and the wet hair—Ashlynn Hughes."

Denver lifted his sunglasses and squinted at a redhead wearing jeans, a wet T-shirt sticking to her body. She'd draped a striped towel over her shoulders.

He snorted. "What did she do, jump off her canoe to get a closer look?"

"She wasn't in a canoe. She saw it while she was swimming." The cop rolled his eyes and held up one hand. "I know, I know. Don't ask me."

"How close are they to hauling it out?" Denver dropped his sunglasses back over his eyes and fished his notebook from his jacket pocket.

"They've been at it for a while. Should be anytime now."

"Thanks, man." Denver picked his way across the rocky shoreline to the woman fluffing the towel through her red locks that glinted with fire every time they caught the sun.

"Ms. Hughes?" He thrust out his hand. Even in bare feet, this tall drink of water almost stood nose to nose with him. "I'm Detective Denver Holt. I understand you're the one who spotted the car and called 9-1-1."

She grasped his hand with a firm slightly damp grip. "I am. I mean it's weird, right? A car in the lake? I wasn't just going to swim on by without telling someone."

His pulse jumped and his gaze behind his dark lenses sharpened. That was a lot of words for a simple yes. "Weird. Definitely weird. Could be an accident, stolen car, insurance fraud. Thanks for calling it in, Ms. Hughes."

Her shoulders beneath the towel slumped as she nodded. "Yeah, I thought so. You can call me Ashlynn."

"Okay… Ashlynn." He flipped open his notebook. "What were you doing in the lake?"

Her blue eyes widened. "What?"

"The lake." He leveled a finger at the body of water. "What were you doing?"

"Swimming." She plucked her soggy T-shirt from her chest, revealing the outline of a one-piece suit beneath. "I went for a swim."

Denver tipped his head back to take in the sky with a few clouds scudding across the sun and hunched into his suit jacket against the sudden breeze. "Not exactly swimming weather."

She flapped her hand toward a few kids paddling and splashing in the water beyond the parking lot. "Tell *them* that. Some of us aren't as…sensitive as you are, Detective."

He cracked a smile. He should've expected feisty with that hair. "So, you decided to drive down to Lake Kawayu and head straight from the parking lot to the water for a swim, and while paddling through the…crystal-clear water you notice a car below you?"

She jutted out one slim hip and wedged a fist on the curve. "Don't put words in my mouth, Detective Holt. I hiked down the trail to get here and jumped in the lake to cool off. While I was swimming, I went vertical to make sure I wasn't going too far out, and my feet skimmed a slab of metal—not what you'd expect to find in a lake."

"Not what I'd expect." He tapped his pen against the notebook. "You ducked down to see what you could see?"

"Yes, and even though the water was cloudy, it was evident that I was floating above a car. I swam back to the shore and called 9-1-1."

"Did you see anything inside the car?" He glanced over his shoulder at the beeping sound from the tow truck. They'd find out soon enough anyway.

She clasped her hands in front of her, knotting her fingers, her sassy demeanor fading as fast as the sun overhead. "I—I didn't get a good look. I didn't want to dive down any deeper, and it was dark and murky."

"Good decision. Did anyone else go into the water after you to take a look?" He made a half-turn to watch the progress of the car as the roof broke the surface of the lake and the water sluiced over the metal.

"I didn't tell anyone what I'd found. I called 9-1-1 and waited for the police. These other people started gathering when the cop car showed up, and then the officer wouldn't let anyone in the water after that." She bit her bottom lip as the dark sedan cleared the water and swung from the pulleys like a bloated fish on the line.

Denver shaded his eyes against the sun glinting off the lake. "Doesn't look like it's been sitting there too long."

She shivered and rubbed her arms. "No, it doesn't."

"Thanks for the information, Ms. Hughes." He stuffed his notebook into his pocket. As he turned, she covered her mouth with both hands.

He stopped. "You don't recognize the car, do you?"

"No, no, of course not."

He strode toward the tow truck, grabbing his cell

phone from his pocket. He took several pictures of the car as it dangled above the lake.

He stood back as the winch settled the vehicle on the shore with a groan, water pouring from its orifices. He borrowed a flashlight from Brooks and crept toward the waterlogged car, which was still hissing and weeping. He leaned toward the windows and aimed the beam of light inside. It illuminated the empty front seat He shifted the focus to the back seat and saw nothing.

He let out a breath and called to one of the divers emerging from the lake, removing his mask. "Anything or…anyone around the car down there?"

"Nope, but the doors were closed and no broken windows, as you can see, so it doesn't look like anyone escaped from the vehicle, either."

"But the water pressure could've closed an open door, right?"

"Could happen."

"Key fob's in the cup holder." Denver pulled on a pair of gloves and tugged on the door handle. The door opened with a whooshing sound. More water gushed from the car, soaking his shoes. He leaned inside and snatched the key fob from the cup holder.

He almost bumped into Ashlynn Hughes as he backed out of the vehicle. She'd followed him beyond the yellow tape.

"Nothing in the car?" Her breathless voice matched her wide eyes and wayward hair.

It was like the shock of finding a submerged car was just hitting her.

"Nothing." He cupped her elbow. "You can move back, Ms. Hughes."

She shuffled back a few steps as he raised his phone to take pictures of the California license plate and the interior. He'd call it in. They still might be able to read the vehicle registration if it hadn't gotten too soggy. The car looked new. Maybe someone had stolen it or abandoned it for insurance fraud. Different scenarios popped into his head as he took pictures. They'd have to get into that trunk, too.

"Are you going to check the trunk?"

The redhead was still hovering, and he swung around, phone in hand. "You really need to step away, Ms. Hughes."

"Ashlynn, and don't you usually open the trunk?" Her shirt had dried, but her teeth chattered, and she pulled the towel tighter around her body.

Officer Brooks huddled close to the rear of the car with a crowbar in his hand. "Do you want me to do the honors?"

"The key fob was in the cup holder." Denver dangled it from his finger. His thumb trembled slightly as he smoothed it across the trunk button on the fob. Then he stabbed it.

The lock clicked and one of the divers, who was standing behind Brooks, let out a sigh. Denver held his breath as he nudged up the trunk with two gloved fingers.

The lid swung high, and Denver's heart slammed against his chest. Looked like he'd got his homicide, after all.

Chapter Two

Ashlynn gagged and stumbled backward, covering her nose and mouth with one hand to ward off the smell emanating from the trunk—part rotting meat, part swamp creature.

Detective Holt turned on her and shouted in her face. "I told you to get back."

And I told you to check the trunk.

She clamped her lips shut and gritted her teeth, which helped keep the nausea at bay, anyway. She ducked under the yellow tape and pressed a fist against her stomach.

Her anonymous tipster had been right. How much of her story should she reveal to Holt, now speaking into his phone?

"Homicide, it's Holt. I went to investigate a car submerged in Lake Kawayu and found a body in the trunk."

Ashlynn narrowed her eyes. The hot detective didn't even work in homicide. As Holt continued to yammer on about license plates and registration,

Ashlynn scanned the crowd that had grown bigger when the tow truck hauled the car to the surface.

Had one of those spectators already known there'd be a car in the lake? Had he or she already known about the body? Was someone watching her? Now that the tipster had proved to be accurate, Ashlynn needed to contact him or her—ask for more.

Sean would know what to do at this point. She'd look through his old exchanges with other informants to see how he'd handled it. This could be her chance to revive *LA Confidential* to its former glory under her brother.

She glanced at the pale flesh in the trunk of the car and her stomach turned. Sean had started the blog to get justice for victims after someone had murdered his friend AJ, and the case had gone cold. She couldn't lose sight of that mission. Sean would want her to get justice for that woman in the car.

And her brother didn't always play by the rules.

She squared her shoulders as Detective Holt marched toward her, his suit jacket flapping in the breeze, revealing a broad chest and flat belly beneath his dress shirt. He stopped on the other side of the tape from her, and she could see herself reflected in his dark glasses.

"Why were you so anxious for me to open the trunk? What were you really doing out here… Ashlynn?"

He'd finally used her first name, and it sounded like a sneer on his lips. She cleared her throat. "I wasn't anxious. I figured you'd be opening the trunk anyway. Right?"

His face reddened. "Of course. I don't need you to tell me how to do my job, but I still don't understand why you were swimming in Lake Kawayu, a body of water more suited to boaters and kids splashing on the shore than serious swimmers."

"Serious? Who said I was a serious swimmer? I hiked almost two miles and fancied a dip in the water to cool off." She clamped her teeth together to stop the tremble rolling through her body. "It's not against the law to swim in this lake. Then my foot hit the submerged car, and I called the police. Why am I in the wrong here? You should be thanking me."

Detective Holt opened his mouth and then snapped it shut with the arrival of a dark sedan, similar to the one the tow truck had just hauled from the lake. Holt held up his index finger instead and said, "Don't go anywhere."

She had no intention of leaving. As he strode toward a tall woman getting out of the car, Ashlynn aimed her phone at the people clustered beyond the yellow tape and started taking pictures. Her tipster could be one of them.

Thirty minutes later, after consulting with the woman from the unmarked police sedan and bagging items from the car, Holt returned to her with a decided spring to his step. How anyone could be in a chipper mood after hovering around that trunk was beyond her, but cops had a different sensibility from civilians. Sean had always had a love-hate relationship with them.

Detective Holt stuffed a hand in his pocket and

pulled out a business card. "Here's my card. Don't hesitate to call me if you remember anything else about the discovery of the car…or why you were swimming in a dirty lake on a day that reached sixty-six degrees tops."

Snatching the card from his fingers, she said, "I gave you all I got, Detective. D-did you identify the victim yet?"

"No." He tipped his sunglasses down to the end of his nose and tagged her with a stare over the top of his lenses. "Fingerprints were hard to get, license plates came back to a different vehicle, so we know they were swapped out, no registration in the glove compartment, and a filed-down VIN."

Her mind got stuck on the image of the victim's fingertips, and she shook her head as if to clear it. He'd surprised her with the details he'd provided— and seemed to surprise himself, as well.

His jaw hardened and he shoved his glasses back into place. "I may be calling you to follow up."

I should be so lucky. She watched his broad shoulders encased by his suit jacket as he returned to the car. While they had been speaking, a coroner's van had shown up at the scene and a few officers had tented the car with a pop-up, blocking the view of the onlookers.

She didn't want to watch the guys in biohazard suits load that body in a bag, anyway. She crouched to pick up her daypack and slung it over one shoulder. Her T-shirt had mostly dried, but the seat of her jeans was still damp. She twisted her hair into a bun and started the trek back down the trail.

Her contact had proved to be accurate about the car and the body. What else did her anonymous source know…and how?

DENVER SPENT ANOTHER HOUR at the crime scene before packing it in and heading back to the Northeast Division. His anger and disgust at discovering that poor woman in the truck of the car tempered his satisfaction with his temporary assignment to Robbery-Homicide to work this case. He'd been on loan to Homicide as a floater before, and had been itching for another opportunity. Too bad the death of that woman had landed him his chance.

On the other hand, he'd do his damnedest to find out who'd killed her and deliver justice to her family. Justice the Portland PD had failed to deliver to his own family when his father was murdered.

Someone had gone to a lot of trouble to disguise the car—swapped out the plates, removed the registration, and filed down the VIN. But all those efforts would prove to be fruitless, as most car manufacturers placed the VIN in a couple of places—some not readily apparent. LAPD's auto theft should be able to figure it out soon enough.

When he got back to the station, he checked in with Captain Fields and then got down to business. Identifying the victim took precedence over everything else right now. He pulled up the database for missing persons in Los Angeles County and narrowed the search based on gender, age and race. Date range would be tricky, as the medical examiner at the scene couldn't pin down anything specific due to the condition of the corpse in the water that had flooded the trunk.

As Denver clicked through the photos and details of the missing women, a hand clamped on his shoulder and he jumped.

Detective Billy Crouch nodded toward the computer. "Heard you're working the case of the woman found in the trunk at Lake Kawayu. What race is she?"

"I'm helping out. It's Detective Marino's case." Denver flicked his fingers at the waifish blond, one of the missing women, peering at them from the monitor. "Caucasian."

Crouch snorted. "If Marino caught the case, that means you'll have a lot of work to do. Anything yet?"

"Not yet and no viable prints from the victim."

"Let me know if you need any help navigating that database... I'm an expert." Crouch twisted his mouth into a grimace before heading out the door.

Crouch obsessively homed in on any case involving a dead woman, as his own sister had been missing for years. If the woman in the trunk had been African American, Crouch would've demanded to see her, no doubt.

Denver could understand that kind of fixation. His father's murder had galvanized his own determination to work Homicide. He didn't need a therapist to figure that one out.

After more than an hour staring at the computer monitor, his eyes began to glaze over. The missing woman on his screen had been gone for three years already. He massaged his temples. How did the families cope with that?

His phone rang and he grabbed it, grateful for the interruption. "Holt."

"Detective Holt, this is Dr. Saleh with the ME Coroner's department. We haven't done an autopsy yet on the victim in the lake, but we do have a preliminary cause of death."

"Go ahead." Denver brought up the file on his computer that contained the details from the case.

"Gunshot wound to the head."

The breath Denver had been holding escaped in a noisy rush. "So, not drowning."

"I did say *preliminary*. Of course, seeing the wound leads us to believe death by firearm, but we can't yet rule out the possibility that someone shot her first, shut her in the trunk and let her drown."

Denver's gut lurched. "All right. Thanks for the call, Dr. Saleh. You'll let me or Detective Marino know when you have the full autopsy?"

The doctor clicked his tongue. "Yes, I just tried calling Detective Marino, but he didn't pick up, and your name was second on the list."

"I'll be sure to let him know. Thanks, again."

When he ended the call with the ME, Denver drummed his fingers on the edge of the keyboard. Crouch had been right about Marino. He had a reputation for laziness, and Denver planned to take advantage of that fact. If he could solve this case without much input from Marino, he might be on the fast track to Robbery-Homicide.

As he thumbed through his notebook to make sure he'd transferred all his information from its pages to his file online, he stopped at Ashlynn Hughes's name. What had she really been doing in that lake? No sensible adult would be swimming laps in Lake Kawayu.

Maybe she'd witnessed the car going into the lake…or something worse, and hadn't wanted to get too involved. But finding the car itself had put her smack in the middle of the investigation. He'd give her a call, have her come into the station. Sitting in an interrogation room seemed to prompt people's memories.

He reached for the phone and stopped when he heard a wail from down the hall. That didn't sound good. He jumped to his feet and followed the sound of the commotion—jagged crying and soothing voices—right into the Robbery-Homicide division.

Clinging to the doorjamb, his gaze swept the room, landing on Crouch sitting on the edge of his desk in front of a red-faced woman flailing her arms in the air.

In contrast to Crouch's low voice, which Denver couldn't hear, the woman cried out, "I know it's her. She's been missing for three days. I've checked everywhere."

Denver's pulse picked up speed and he took a few steps into the room, raising his eyebrows at Crouch.

"Here's the detective working the case, Mrs. Edmunds." Crouch cupped his hand and gestured him forward. "I'll let you talk to him."

Denver squared his shoulders. Nobody liked this part of Homicide. On his way to Billy and the woman, he pulled out a chair next to an empty desk. "Mrs. Edmunds, I'm Detective Holt. Why don't you take a seat, and we can talk?"

He did have photos of the dead girl in the trunk, but he'd never show those to a mother—whether the picture was of her daughter or not.

Mopping her face with a handful of tissues he was sure she'd gotten from Billy, Mrs. Edmunds walked toward him with a jerky gait. When she sat, he wiped his own hands on the thighs of his slacks. If he could be half as good as Billy at this, he'd ace this encounter.

"Start at the beginning, Mrs. Edmunds. What's your daughter's name?"

"Tiana Fuller. H-her father and I are divorced, and I remarried."

"You say she's been missing for three days? Did you report her disappearance before this?" He hadn't seen a Tiana Fuller or Edmunds in the database this afternoon.

"I'm reporting it now." Her gazed shifted to Billy, now logging off his computer, his head cocked, listening to their conversation. "My husband and I were out of town. We drove down to San Diego to visit his aunt, who'd had a fall. Tiana is twenty-one. S-she lives in Long Beach, near campus. She's just home for spring break and to housesit for us, so we left her on her own. We didn't realize she was missing until we came home this afternoon and couldn't reach her. I thought at first she might've gone back to her place in Long Beach."

"Were you in touch with her while you were in San Diego?"

"We exchanged a few texts the first day. She didn't answer later texts, but Tiana's been living on her own for two years at school. We didn't want to… hover." She dropped her head and balled the wad of tissues in her fist. "We should've. We should've come home sooner."

"And you're here now because you heard about the woman found at Lake Kawayu?"

She nodded without lifting her head.

"What makes you think this is Tiana? Did she frequent that area?"

Her head shot up and she pinned him with her wild, red-rimmed eyes. "I just know it. I have a feeling."

Denver massaged his stiff neck. Any parent of a missing child would feel the same after learning of the discovery of a dead woman. "Do you have a picture of Tiana, Mrs. Edmunds?"

Sniffling, she dug into her purse, eager to be doing something at last. With a trembling hand, she held out a picture of a young woman with light brown hair and a turned-up nose.

Denver swallowed. The woman in the trunk had brownish-blond hair and a slender build like Tiana's—

but so did a lot of young women. He took the photo from her and studied the face, keeping his own impassive as Mrs. Edmund's gaze probed him.

She croaked. "Is it her? Is she the girl in the trunk?"

"I can't say right now, Mrs. Edmunds. Do you have any idea what she was wearing when she last went out? What car she'd be driving?"

"Her car's at home." She shredded the tissues. "I don't understand why you can't tell me if she's the one in that trunk."

His gaze darted to Billy, who was taking his sweet time logging off and packing up his stuff.

Billy cleared his throat. "We can't make a positive ID based on just a picture, Mrs. Edmunds. Leave the photo of your daughter with Detective Holt. The next step is to provide us with your daughter's DNA—hair from her brush, toothbrush—something like that."

She bit her bottom lip. "You can't show me pictures of the dead girl? I'd know Tiana anywhere."

"That's not advisable at this time, Mrs. Edmonds." Denver shifted forward to meet her gaze. She had to know what he meant. "As Detective Crouch said, we want to wait for a positive ID through DNA first."

"Okay." She slumped in her chair.

She obviously hadn't been looking forward to the task of collecting her daughter's DNA. What made her think she could look at a picture of a dead body that had been submerged in water?

Once Denver got more information from her and

gave her his card, he walked her to the exit and then jogged upstairs to talk to Billy.

Denver leaned against a desk and crossed his arms. "Thanks for rescuing me."

"You would've figured it out." Billy hitched his bag over his shoulder. "Who found the car, anyway? Doesn't seem like a boater would run into it or hit it with an oar. You can't see anything in that lake from the air."

"It was a swimmer. She went vertical, and her foot brushed the top of the car."

Billy's jaw dropped. "A swimmer in *that* lake? I mean, I know little kids like to splash around the shore, but swim?"

"That was my reaction. I was just going to call the witness to invite her in tomorrow and grill her a little more. She seemed...vague."

"Same age as the victim?"

"Older, but not by much. Different last name, of course, so no link there. Hughes. Ashlynn Hughes is her name."

Billy whistled through his teeth. "Oh, boy."

"What?" Denver pushed off the desk, his heart pounding. "Do you know her?"

"Not personally, but I know who she is, and I knew who her brother was."

"What?" Denver shook his head, pain lancing the back of his neck. "Her brother? What are you talking about?"

"You know the true crime blog, *LA Confidential*? Her brother, Sean Hughes, wrote that blog until he was murdered, and his sister's picked up where he left off."

Denver clenched his jaw. Know it? He not only knew about *LA Confidential*, that blog and Sean Hughes had made his life a living hell.

Chapter Three

Ashlynn wedged her feet against the edge of the coffee table and flipped open the computer in her lap. Holding her breath, she navigated to the private message area connected to the blog. If readers didn't want to post something publicly to the comments section, they could message her directly. That's how her anonymous tipster had sent her the first message about a car in Lake Kawayu—with a body in the trunk.

She scanned the direct messages, skimming over the ones asking her to take on a case, tearing up over the ones with condolences on Sean's death, and deleting the marriage pitches and indecent proposals. Had Sean gotten those?

She slumped against the couch and took a sip of green tea, lolling the mellow flavor on her tongue. Nothing new from her source. He or she must've seen the discovery of the car and the body in the lake. It had been all over the news. Detective Denver Holt's face had been all over the news. A girl could get lost in those chocolate-brown eyes.

She took a quick gulp of tea that went down the wrong way, and she hacked and wiped her eyes. That's what she got for straying from her purpose.

Neither Holt nor the news reports had mentioned her name, so maybe her tipster didn't realize she'd been the one to report the car. She scooped in a breath and poised her hand over the keyboard. She'd have to remedy that and keep those tips coming. The more firsthand knowledge she had of the case, the more she could engage her readers—and take them with her on to her next adventure.

At the time of Sean's death, he'd been working on morphing his blog into a podcast. She'd been helping him with the project, never imagining she'd have to go it alone.

She flexed her fingers and typed in a response to the initial message, thanking her source for the tip and letting him—her?—know that she'd been responsible for finding the car and reporting it.

She hit the return key with a flourish and watched the blank space below her message. Sighing, she wrapped her hands around her mug. Sean had been so much better at this than she was proving to be. Sean had been so much better at most things.

She slid her laptop onto the couch and took her cup to the kitchen. As she rinsed it under the faucet, her cell phone buzzed. She hightailed it back to the living room and swooped down on the phone as it vibrated on the coffee table.

She screwed up one side of her face. She usually didn't answer calls from unknown numbers, but she was operating in a different world now. She answered, willing the trepidation from her voice. "Hello?"

The man on the other end dispensed with the niceties. "You are a liar and a fraud. What do you think you're playing at?"

Ashlynn pressed a palm against her skittering heart. "What? Who is this?"

"You know damned well this is Detective Holt, and I know who you are. *LA Confidential.*" He spat out the words so forcefully, she twitched.

The edges of the phone dug into her hand as she gripped it. She'd been expecting this. Sooner or later, Holt would've become aware that she was featuring this case on the blog. She'd just hoped it would've been later.

"I didn't lie." Not really. She sank to the couch, her knees hitting the coffee table. "I was swimming in the lake and I discovered the car."

He gave her something like a growl over the phone. "That's a lie. You pretended like you were there by chance when you went in that water specifically to look for that car."

She needed Sean's bravado about now. "It doesn't matter why I was in the water, does it? I found the car and did the right thing."

"Who told you about the car? How'd you know it was there? Why didn't you call the cops when you got the tip?"

"Well, I'm just not going to answer those questions. This was confidential, anonymous, information."

"You're not a psychiatrist or an attorney." The sneer in his voice slid through the phone and slithered under her skin.

"I'm a journalist." She enunciated each syllable.

"Is that what you call it? Encouraging online sleuths to launch their own investigations. Hampering the police. Smearing people's names." He stopped the tirade and took a big breath.

She could picture his dark, narrowed eyes, flushed cheeks, thin line of his lips. She shivered, glad they were on the phone and not across from each other.

"Whatever your opinion of journalists, we need to protect our sources." She sawed at her bottom lip with her teeth. "Besides, I couldn't tell you, anyway. The tip was anonymous. I don't know who this person is."

"You got the tip on your computer?"

"I'm not answering that."

"We can trace activity on your computer."

She muttered a curse. It hadn't taken him long to trick her. "You could trace it if you had my computer. You don't."

He lowered his voice and almost purred in her ear. "Don't you want justice for this young woman?"

She blinked. He didn't fight fair. "O-of course, I do. Look, I don't have any information that's going to help you find her killer…"

He heard the pause. "Yet. Is that what you mean? You don't have anything yet, but you hope to solve this case—you and your wannabe detective minions. Butt out, Hughes."

He elongated the *S* at the end of her name, sounding like a snake.

"You do your job, Detective Holt, and I'll do mine. Maybe the twain will meet at some point, and we can help each other."

"Don't count on it."

He ended the call before she could form a retort. Instead, she said it to the empty room. "Whew, someone woke up on the wrong side of the cage."

She'd known Detective Holt wouldn't be thrilled that she planned to feature this case on *LA Confidential*, but she hadn't expected him to get so mad about it.

From what she understood about him, he didn't typically work Robbery-Homicide. If he were on loan for this case, an arrest would make him look good—better than he already did. Maybe she could help him. Maybe they could help each other. She'd have to get past that wall first.

Ashlynn tucked a leg beneath her and dragged the computer into her lap. She entered his name in a search engine and her eyes popped at the number of entries. This had to be him. Who named their kid Denver?

She clicked on a promising link and read the article with a sick feeling in her belly. Denver's father had been murdered in Oregon years ago. They'd never found his father's killer.

She clicked on a more recent link and smacked her hand to her forehead. *LA Confidential*, her brother, had done an investigation into the murder of Denver's father and had insinuated that his mother was the killer.

"Oh, Sean." She covered her face with her hands. Denver Holt didn't just hate blogs—he hated *her* blog and her dead brother. Could she blame him?

She accessed Sean's archives for the blog. Why had her brother even dug into the Holt family tragedy in Portland? *LA Confidential* usually stayed true to its name and focused on crimes in Los Angeles. It's not like this city had a shortage.

As she scrolled through the archives, her computer dinged, indicating a new private message on the blog. She navigated to the in-box and her hand trembled just a little when she clicked on the message.

She read it aloud. "'Knew I could count on you. Have more but don't want to be traced through these messages. Meet me tonight.'"

The blood pounded in her temples. This is exactly how Sean had lost his life. He'd gone to meet a source…and wound up dead.

She massaged the back of her neck. That was different. Sean had made contact with a serial killer. He was acting as the conduit between a murderer and the cops who were trying to stop him. This was a concerned citizen, afraid to go to the police, trying to get justice for a murder victim. Wasn't it?

Sean's voice echoed in her head, warning her that she'd never succeed if she weren't willing to take risks. Her parents' voices chimed in, predicting she'd never continue the blog's popularity without Sean.

She pushed her hair from her face and asked for a name. A message popped up immediately: Angel.

Did her silent partner mean to put her at ease with that? Angel could be a man or a woman, or could stand for guardian angel. Ashlynn asked for the meeting details, already more than half sure she'd be going through with this.

Angel suggested Venice, the slice of Washington Boulevard near the pier, loaded with bars and restaurants. She'd walk along the sidewalk and Angel would approach her with the phrase *Try the mai tai at Tahiti Nui*. Tahiti Nui was a bar in the area, so that made sense, but not something a complete stranger would say to someone.

Ashlynn ended the exchange with a description of the clothing she'd be wearing, but when Angel assured her she knew what Ashlynn looked like, a whisper of fear tickled the back of her neck.

She sat for a few minutes staring at the screen. Could she trust Angel? Why not? There was no reason for Angel or anyone else to want to harm her. She didn't know anything about the case of the woman in the trunk...not yet. Angel wouldn't be probing her for information, as Angel was the one providing all the tips. Ashlynn was just a mouthpiece. Wasn't that what Sean always maintained?

Until he'd become the mouthpiece for a serial killer and lost his life.

Ashlynn bounded from the couch and snagged a denim jacket from the closet by the front door of the duplex she rented in Culver City. She didn't live far from Venice, but she didn't want to be late. If Angel didn't see her right away, she might think she'd gotten cold feet. Ashlynn didn't think she could muster up her courage again for this meeting.

She slung her purse across her body and tucked a canister of pepper spray in the outside pocket—just in case Angel was no angel.

As she closed her door, she waved to her duplex neighbors just pulling their car into the spot next to hers. Niles was a software engineer, and his girlfriend, whose name she'd forgotten, had just moved in with him a few months ago. They clambered from their car, weighed down with bags of food from the local Chinese place and waved back.

They knew what she did. Knew about *LA Confidential* and what had happened to Sean. They didn't hold it against her—of course, the blog had never accused their parents of murder. She'd tried to dismiss Denver from her mind, but she hadn't been successful. Even without the blog stuff, she'd have a hard time forgetting Denver Holt—tall, dark, handsome and…ornery. She couldn't help herself. She'd always had a weakness for guys who were hard to get—or at least played hard to get.

She'd make a more concerted effort to block him from her mind, as he was probably married with a few kids and, well, he hated her. There was hard to get and then there was near impossible. She'd slot him into the latter category and forget about him.

She cruised west into Venice and the indigo sky

that hung above the ocean, soaking up the last of the sun's rays that still floated on the water.

Parking was no picnic in Venice, and Ashlynn circled twice before waiting for a couple getting into their car. When they vacated the spot, she wheeled in.

She stepped out onto the sidewalk and adjusted her purse. She'd arrived fifteen minutes before the appointed meeting time and could squeeze in a stroll to the pier and back before expecting Angel to approach her.

She strode down Washington to the pier, looking straight ahead. She didn't want it to seem as if she were looking for someone, and she didn't want to catch the eye of any of the homeless people who mingled with the rest of crowd scooting in and out of the bars and restaurants that lined the street.

At least Angel had suggested a populated location, although Angel must've been wary of any cameras catching them inside one of the businesses. It sort of made sense to Ashlynn, which was one of the reasons she'd agreed to pounding the sidewalk aimlessly until Angel approached her with the code phrase.

Her gaze flicked toward Tahiti Nui, patrons with drinks in their hands crowding the patio in the front. Angel knew this area, unless she'd just looked it up on the internet. You could discover anything on the internet—including why the hot cop you'd immediately crushed on hated you.

She sauntered to the beginning of the old pier and inhaled the salty air. A few fishermen in sil-

houette packed up their gear, and an old man carefully navigated the wooden slats. She gulped in a few
more breaths and turned to face the boulevard where
someone calling herself Angel awaited.

She crossed the parking lot and started walking
down the north side of the street. When she reached
Pacific, she crossed to the other side of the street
and headed back toward the pier. Before the parking
lot as she crossed back over, a homeless woman approached her with her dirt-encrusted hand held out.

"Spare change?"

"Sorry, not today." Ashlynn moved past her and,
out of the corner of her eye, saw the homeless woman
turn in her direction to follow her. Great. She should
probably just slip her a dollar to get rid of her.

As Ashlynn plunged her hand in her purse, the
woman whispered, "You should try the mai tai at
Tahiti Nui."

Ashlynn spun around. "What did you say?"

The woman opened her mouth in a toothless grin
and crooked her finger. "Try the mai tai at Tahiti Nui."

Stumbling after the shambling woman, Ashlynn
asked, "Who are you?"

This couldn't be Angel, could it? Where would a
woman like this get a computer? The library? It made
sense. A transient might be more likely to witness
a crime without someone noticing her. A transient
might be less likely to contact the police for fear of
being dismissed, or worse. Did homeless people read
LA Confidential? Again, they could have access to

computers at the library. Anyone could get access to technology today.

The homeless woman didn't turn right onto the sidewalk. She crossed the parking lot and started down Speedway.

Ashlynn hesitated. She didn't want to go this way. They were supposed to stay in a well-lit, crowded area. She licked her lips. "Hold on."

Sand scuffled on the ground to her right and a shadow loomed over her. She clawed for the pepper spray from the side of her purse and as her fingers curled around the canister, something whacked the back of her head.

She dropped to her knees. Dizzy and nauseous, she waited for the next blow that would end her life—just like Sean's.

Chapter Four

With adrenaline coursing through his veins, Denver broke into a jog and rounded the corner of Speedway, slipping and sliding on the loose sand. Ashlynn lay crumpled on the ground and a dark figure sprinted into the night.

"Hey!" Denver took a few steps toward the fleeing person but heard Ashlynn moan behind him. He cranked his head over his shoulder and skidded to a stop on the gritty pavement as a transient poked Ashlynn with an umbrella.

Denver roared. "Stop that, unless you want to wind up behind bars."

The homeless guy backed off and melted into the shadows.

Denver crouched beside Ashlynn. "Are you all right? What happened?"

Her long eyelashes fluttered and she opened one eye. "What are you doing here?"

"I'll get to that later." He wound an arm beneath her and hoisted her to a sitting position, propping her up against the dirty wall of the building. He hoped she wouldn't notice the stains. "Are you injured?"

She rubbed the back of her head, her fingers showing traces of blood. "Someone hit me on the head."

"That homeless woman you were following?" His gaze darted left and right, but he didn't see any sign of the female transient.

"How do you know…?" She shook her head. "Not her. Someone came at me from between the two buildings. Hit me with something."

"An umbrella?"

"Umbrella?" She wrinkled her nose and he noticed a few freckles scattered across her skin. "Heavier than an umbrella. Felt like a brick. Is it bleeding badly?"

Leaning over her, he parted some strands of her hair, sticky with blood. His fingers traced a small bump. "You have a lump on your head, but it's not gushing blood. I'll call the paramedics."

"No." She grabbed his arm as he reached for the phone in his pocket. "I don't need any medical attention. Just some ice and maybe a drink—no mai tais at Tahiti Nui."

He cocked his head. She must still be confused and dizzy. "You sure you don't want to get treated?"

"I'm sure." She flattened a hand against the stucco wall and then snatched it away. "God, this is gross. Can we get out of here?"

He helped her up and she staggered against him. Tucking an arm around her waist, he led her back to the street, the lights and the people. What the hell had she been thinking, following that woman onto Speedway in the dark?

He walked her past Tahiti Nui and steered her across the street to Venice Whaler. They bypassed the hostess and he settled Ashlynn in a booth at the edge of the bar. "Do you want to use the restroom to clean that wound? It looks like it stopped bleeding. I'll get some ice from the waitress and a plastic bag. What do you want to drink? Anything but a mai tai?"

"Get me an Irish whiskey—Jameson, neat."

He raised his brows as she scooted out of the booth. Not what he'd expected, but she did look like an Irish lass with all that red hair. He kept his eyes on the dark recess where Ashlynn had disappeared—just in case someone followed her.

A waitress flicked a couple of napkins onto the table. "What can I get you?"

"Jameson, neat, and whatever light beer you have. Can you also get me a small plastic bag with ice?"

When the waitress quirked her eyebrow, he explained. "My friend bumped her head."

"Oh, is she okay?"

Denver tipped his head at Ashlynn making her way back to the table. "She's fine."

The waitress touched Ashlynn's arm. "I'll bring you that ice. Do you need anything else?"

"He ordered the whiskey?"

"He did."

"Thanks, I'm good." She slid into the booth across from Denver. "Now that my head is somewhat clear, you can start talking."

"Me?" He jabbed a finger into his chest. "Why

don't you start by telling me what you were doing down here?"

"You obviously followed me or—" she narrowed her eyes "—whatever. You go first."

He held up his hands in surrender. "You got me. That's all there is to my story. I followed you here."

"From my house? You know where I live?" She winced and squeezed her eyes closed briefly.

"I'm a cop." He tapped the side of his head. "Is that wound giving you trouble?"

"Hurts, but I'm fine. You looked me up after you yelled at me on the phone and then drove out to my house to…what? What did you hope to see?"

"Exactly what I did see." He splayed his hands on the table, touching his thumbs. "You, out on some fool's errand. Just like—"

The waitress appeared just in time to stop him from blurting out something insensitive. A serial killer had murdered her brother. He didn't need anyone to remind him what it felt like to lose a family member to murder.

He took a gulp of beer and toyed with the corner of a napkin. "You need to be careful."

Ashlynn took a tentative sip of her whiskey, and she still sniffed. "I know what happened to your father, and I know my brother covered his case in *LA Confidential*. I'm sorry."

His hand jerked and his beer frothed over the side. "Are you? Isn't that what you bloggers and podcasters do? Go after cold cases and find a killer—even if you're ruining people's lives?"

"I'm not sorry that he featured the case on his blog." She traced her fingertip along the rim of her glass. "I'm sorry you lost your father that way."

He clenched his teeth. Can't accuse this woman of soft-pedaling anything. He usually liked that, didn't he? He took a deep breath and another deep drink.

"I'm sorry about your brother, too. Losing a family member like that messes with your mind. I know it's no consolation to you, but at least you know who killed him. My father's case is still cold—despite your brother's efforts to implicate my mom."

"I had assumed it was the copycat who killed my brother after tempting him with being his contact with the LAPD, but it was really The Player, who'd objected to his copycat working with a true crime blogger. That was a shock." She hugged herself. "Gave me the creeps."

"And this doesn't?" He flicked a finger at the window that looked out over the beach. "Is someone giving you a heads-up about this case? How do you know it's not the killer of that girl in the trunk? How do you know he's not just toying with you? Hoping for some publicity?"

The skin around Ashlynn's luscious mouth turned white and she took another sip of whiskey—not so tentative this time. Her blue eyes watered, and she dabbed her nose with a napkin.

"Who said I was meeting anyone here about the case? I came out to Venice for a walk and a drink." She lifted her glass and the light caught the amber liquid as it sloshed up the sides. "Someone decided to conk me on the head and mug me."

He narrowed his eyes. "That's the way you want to play it? Clicks or whatever you're after are more important than finding the killer of this girl?"

She swirled her drink. "I don't have anything to give you, Detective—no evidence, no clues. I can't solve this case for you."

"You got that right." He smacked his hand on the table, rattling the glasses. "So don't even try."

AFTER ESCAPING DETECTIVE HOLT's dark stare and smoldering anger, Ashlynn slumped in the seat of her car, wedging the bag of ice against her bump with the headrest. She'd been annoyed that Denver had followed her, but he'd probably saved her life. Had she thanked him for that?

She'd been too busy trying to dismiss his suspicions that her contact was just some weirdo looking for publicity…or worse. She couldn't deny that her tipster had just led her into a very dangerous situation.

She tapped her phone and navigated to the blog, which still displayed her wrap-up to the Reed Dufrain case. Her lips turned down at the number of blog visits. You were only as good as your current case—and now she had one. She still had to write and post her first entry for the girl in the lake, but at least she had a name for the case: "The Girl in the Lake."

Now, if only her person of contact wasn't trying to kill her.

She glanced at the empty message in-box and then sighed and started the car. Sean had made it look so easy. But then, he'd made everything look easy.

As she pulled out of her metered parking space, she glanced in her rearview mirror. She'd made it laughably easy for Denver to follow her here. She hadn't once checked for a tail on the way over.

And when had Detective Holt become Denver in her mind? Probably when she was mooning over his dark, liquid eyes across a couple of drinks. She still didn't know if he was married, but a surreptitious glance at his left hand said no, or maybe he didn't like rings.

Would he be chasing after witnesses on his off hours if he had a wife at home? If he were hers, she wouldn't let him out of her sight. She huffed through her nose. That's why her previous relationship had ended—too needy, too clingy. Who wouldn't be with parents like hers?

At least she had both of her parents. Denver's eyes had shimmered with loss when he'd talked about his father's murder—and her brother had added to his pain by suggesting Denver's mother had had something to do with the death.

She cruised up Venice Boulevard, back to her duplex, her eyes darting between her rearview and side mirrors. It had occurred to her there might be others who could be following her; others who meant her more harm than Denver—not that he posed any threat to her. He just wanted his case back, and whatever info she could give him. She could use that to her advantage. He wasn't a detective in LAPD's Robbery-Homicide division—but oh, he wanted to be.

Ashlynn swung into the driveway next to Niles's car. As she exited her vehicle, she grabbed the bag of ice.

She fumbled with her key and, once inside, made a beeline for her kitchen. Dumping out the half-melted ice in the sink, she refilled the bag from her freezer. She downed an ibuprofen with some water and scooped up her laptop with one hand.

Let's see how her tipster wriggled out of this one. She brought up the blog messages and asked Angel what the hell had just happened.

Sipping her water, Ashlynn clicked back and forth between Sean's archives and the blog messages until a ding indicated a new message. She read the explanation from Angel, with a hand at her throat.

Angel insisted she'd been followed and hadn't wanted to put Ashlynn in danger, so she'd melted away without approaching her. They went back and forth, as Ashlynn described what had happened to her, including the code words the homeless woman had uttered—leaving out the part about Denver coming to her rescue.

The fact that the transient had known the phrase freaked out Angel. She couldn't understand how that had happened, unless someone had hacked into her computer. As soon as Angel expressed that thought, she signed off.

Ashlynn nestled her fingers in her hair to trace the small bump on her head. Could she trust Angel? If someone had followed Angel, or had hacked into her computer, that someone knew she had information about the woman in the trunk, and she'd already put herself in danger. Now Angel had put Ashlynn in danger, too. She and Angel had never made contact in Venice, so the person who'd attacked her must've recognized her. Ashlynn had told Angel what she'd be wearing. She must've been easy enough to spot. If Angel were telling the truth, she had been hacked. How could Ashlynn hope to get anything more from her?

Maybe Denver was right. She should give up the whole thing. Who was she kidding? She didn't have Sean's talent, his drive, his courage.

She shoved the computer from her lap and put the glass in the dishwasher. She'd hang on to the bag of ice and give it another ten minutes before she went to bed.

She toed off her running shoes in the bedroom and crossed the floor to the master bath in her stockinged feet. She pushed open the door and blinked in the bright light.

As if in slow motion, her gaze tracked from the lipstick cap on the floor, to the open tube on the vanity, to the letters in red scarlet slashed across her mirror.

Find Another Case.

Chapter Five

After receiving Ashlynn's frantic call about a warning on her mirror, Denver swore as he gunned it on the freeway. He should've followed her home. It's not like she would've known. He'd followed her to Venice tonight on a hunch, and she hadn't noticed him.

He'd had a hunch when she'd set off for her place tonight, too, but he hadn't followed through. After that attack in Venice, he'd known she'd put herself in a sticky situation—and now someone had broken into her house and scribbled a message on her bathroom mirror. Gutsy.

He careered down the off-ramp and ran a few red lights to reach her. When he rolled up her street, he saw the dome light in her car parked in the driveway. She'd been home for almost an hour before she'd discovered the message in the bathroom. The perpetrator would be long gone by now, but he could understand her reluctance to wait inside like a sitting duck.

As he pulled to the curb across the street, Ashlynn shot out of her car and waited on the sidewalk, practically hopping from foot to foot. She started talking before he was halfway across the road.

"Someone broke into my place. I don't know how they got in because as soon as I saw the message on my bathroom mirror, I fled. I don't know if they're still there, hiding."

"Good idea." His forehead creased. "Why didn't you call the police?"

"I did. I called you." She tipped her head at him, making him feel ten feet tall that he'd been her go-to guy.

He had an idea why she hadn't called 9-1-1. When he reached her, she spun around, leading the way to her house. He put a hand on her shoulder. "You can wait out here, if you want."

Her red hair flicked as she glanced over her shoulder. "I feel safe now that you're here."

Did she actually bat her eyelashes? And what was with all the compliments when, two hours ago, she couldn't even thank him for rescuing her from a street attack?

He kept a few paces behind her, not intentionally to watch her hips sway, but that was an added bonus. When she reached the door and unlocked it, he nudged her to the side and withdrew his weapon. "Let me go in first."

Her eyes widened for a second and she held up a canister of pepper spray. "I was going to use this, but that's much more effective."

He eased open the door and stepped into a small entryway, the kitchen branching off in one direction, a hallway in the other, and the living room spread before him.

"I'll check the windows." He tugged on the two snug windows in the kitchen, and studied the one in the living room. She'd locked up tight.

"Do you ever leave this unlocked?" As he walked up to the sliding-glass door that led to a small patio and grassy area, he noticed the drapes puckering inward. He whipped them aside. "Hello."

"What?" She'd been right on his heels and bumped into his back when he stopped.

With his fingertip in the air, he traced the square of glass cut from her door, right next to the handle and the lock. "He got in this way. I take it you don't have a lock on the track of the slider."

Clutching his arm, she bent forward to inspect the intruder's handiwork. "He used some sort of glass-cutter to cut and lift that square out, and then reached in to unlock the door."

"Doesn't even have to be that fancy. Someone can just smash through the glass and unlock it if it's the only lock on the door." He jerked his thumb at what must be the wall she shared with her neighbors. "Probably didn't want to make that much noise."

"Damn." She kicked the metal door track with her bare foot. "I had a little screw-on device on here at one point."

"Weren't you in the living room before you discovered the note in the bathroom? You didn't notice the air coming in through this door?"

"The drapes were already closed, and I was sit-

ting on the couch with my back to that door. Never
even noticed it." She folded her arms and hunched
her shoulders. "I guess I should've checked all the
windows and doors myself after what happened tonight. I didn't think… I mean I didn't see anyone
following me from Venice. Whoever this is, knows
where I live."

"Unless he's followed you before…maybe home
from the lake that day."

"So, now that we know how he gained entrance to
my house—" she crooked her finger at him "—I'll
show you the scary part."

As she led him through her bedroom, he skirted
the king-size bed with one corner of the blue floral
bedspread turned down, and his gaze flicked toward
a pile of clothes on a chair, a lacy bra dangling off
the arm.

She pushed open the bathroom door with a flourish.
"He used my lipstick and didn't bother to put it away
when he was finished. I actually noticed the lipstick
before the words on my mirror."

The red warning leaped out at him immediately—
block letters, no misspellings, intentional or otherwise, and no regard for Ashlynn's lipstick.

"I hope that wasn't your favorite color." He
nudged the cap on the floor with the toe of his shoe.
"Do you have a plastic bag?"

She loosened her grip on the doorjamb and ran a
hand through her wavy hair that curled at the ends.
"You mean like to bag this up as evidence?"

"I doubt we'll find any prints but yours, but it's

worth a try." He met her eyes in the mirror. Two chips of ice stared back.

"I'm not reporting this." She folded her arms at her chest, crossing one leg over the other. She looked like a pretzel.

"You sort of did report it." He spread out his arms. "As you pointed out earlier, I am a cop."

Her gaze dropped to his backside, and he felt a coiling response in his belly. "You're not wearing your cop clothes and, besides, you're LAPD. The last time I looked out my window, I lived in Culver City. We have our own police force."

He turned to face her. "We work with Culver City all the time. I'm sure they'd be more than happy to help out with a homicide in LA."

"Who said anything about a homicide in LA?" She gave him a bug-eyed stare and an exaggerated shrug, like a cartoon character. "I got scared because someone broke into my place and scrawled a message on my bathroom mirror. I did what any girl would do who had the phone number of a hunky cop at her fingertips—called him."

She thought he was hunky? Did women even say hunky anymore? He stiffened his back and just managed to avoid puffing out his chest. "You're telling me you called me so you could check out my ass?"

"I was not…" Her cheeks matched her hair, and she knew it. She took a deep breath. "I called you because your number was handy and I was scared… and you already saved me once tonight."

He rubbed the back of his neck. "Let's start over.

You are planning to feature this case on *LA Confidential*, and someone is already warning you off. I checked the blog, and you haven't posted anything about this case. How did your intruder know to warn you off? I think we can agree that the attack in Venice was another warning. How did that person know you were going to be down on Washington tonight?"

She drummed her fingers against the door. "Let's get out of the bathroom. Coffee? Water? Beer?"

"Did this turn into a social call?"

"Friendly business." She backed away from the bathroom. "I'll even get the baggie for the lipstick."

He had no choice but to follow her. Hell, even if he had a choice, he'd follow her.

She gestured toward the couch. "Have a seat, or help yourself to something to drink first. I'll bag the lipstick and cap, and don't worry, I won't touch either one."

She rummaged in a kitchen drawer and hustled back to the bedroom, a small plastic bag stuck to her fingertips.

Denver took her place in the kitchen and opened the fridge. He grabbed a soda from the top shelf. He could use a little caffeine right now but couldn't face coffee. He didn't want to be too wired for this friendly business meeting, but he needed to be on his toes.

Ashlynn sashayed back into the living room, swinging the baggie with the lipstick tube and cap. "Here you go. Just don't do anything official with it because I'm not reporting this break-in."

Cocking his head, Denver asked, "Why not?"

"What happens in the blogging world, stays in the blogging world. I don't want any official record of what I'm up to." She pretended to turn a key at her lips.

He supposed this was what he'd signed up for when he agreed to work with her. He circled his finger in the air. "Did you ever check to see if anything was missing?"

"Just made sure my laptop was still here—that's it. I don't have any expensive jewelry stashed away, no bundles of cash, no fancy electronic devices, and no guns—yet."

Denver rolled his eyes. "God, help us. I got a soda for myself. Did you want one?"

"I'm good." She dropped the baggie on the coffee table next to where he was perching on the arm of the couch. "What can you do with that…unofficially?"

"I can get someone to run prints…unofficially." He answered her raised eyebrows. "I know people."

"I'll bet you do." She took the other end of the sofa, bracing her back against the arm and stretching out her long legs toward him.

He glanced at her toes wiggling in her socks and slid down the arm so that he landed on a cushion of the couch, her feet inches from his lap. "What business could we possibly have together?"

She pulled her knees to her chest, wrapping one arm around them. "I need a case…and you need a case. This could be it for both of us."

His nostrils flared as some emotion thumped in

his chest. Anger? Shame? Excitement? He couldn't
even ID it, himself.

He ran his hands across his face, his day-old beard
scratching his palms. "You're suggesting we help
each other—I keep you apprised of the investigation and you give me what you're getting from the
readers of your blog."

She nodded, blue eyes sparkling. Anyone looking
in at her might think they were discussing wedding
plans instead of murder.

He held up one finger and growled more fiercely
than he'd intended. "I see one problem with that."

She flashed him her pearly whites. "Only one?"

"One major problem." He cleared his throat and
took a sip of soda, the bubbles rushing to his nose.
"The information I'd be giving you would be accurate. The stuff you'd be passing off to me...garbage."

She tipped her feet back on her heels and tapped
them together. "Did I find garbage in Lake Kawayu?
No. I found a car with a body in the trunk. Would
you have found that body without me? Doubt it."

"Which brings us back to the beginning." He
jabbed his finger into the couch at the edge of her
toes, where the gesture lost all effectiveness as his
finger sank into the cushion. "How did you know
where to find the car? Why did you go to Venice
tonight?"

"If I tell you, can you keep it to yourself? It's all
garbage, anyway, right? Lunatics out in cyber land
who want to play detective. If word gets around in
law enforcement circles that I'm cooperating with

a cop, I might not get any more information. If we keep this hush-hush between us, I might still get the info, I can feed it to you and you only, you can give me a little inside story and—" she clapped her hands "—I've got a blog worth reading and you're the hotshot detective who solved the case. That's what we both want, isn't it? Justice for that woman in the trunk?"

Denver circled his fingers around the can of soda and squeezed in one side of the aluminum. How pathetic and obvious he must've come across. Playing at being a homicide detective without really being a homicide detective. Ashlynn had spotted his desperation a mile off, must've smelled it coming from him in waves.

What did he have to lose?

He thrust out his hand. "Justice for the girl in the trunk."

A LITTLE THRILL fluttered through her veins as she clasped Denver's warm, strong hand. "It's a deal, Detective."

"If we're going to be working with each other, you can start calling me Denver." He squeezed her hand before releasing it.

She settled back against the arm of the couch, failing to mention she'd already been calling him Denver in her head. "I'll try."

His eyebrows knitted. "Start now. How did you know that car was going to be in the lake with a body inside?"

He wanted to get right down to business. She took a deep breath. "I got a tip on my blog."

"I figured that. How?" He hunched forward, elbows on knees. "Someone posted on the blog for everyone else to see?"

"I—Sean had a private message feature on the blog. People can hit the message icon and contact me directly, without anyone else seeing it."

He rubbed his knuckles against his stubble. "More private than emailing you because the person can mask his or her email address."

"Exactly. Sean thought that method would encourage more tips—and it has."

Nodding toward the laptop on the table, he asked, "Can you show me the message?"

"Yes." She swung her legs off the couch and flipped open her computer. She accessed the blog, clicked on her private messages, and scrolled back to her first contact with Angel.

She jabbed her finger at the screen. "That's the first time she contacted me."

"'She'?" He pulled the computer into his lap, forcing her to scoot closer to him if she wanted to see what he was reading.

"She has since identified herself as Angel."

"Angel. *Angel.*" He pronounced the name the second time in Spanish. "Could be a Latino dude."

"Could be, but I have a feeling this is a woman."

He squinted at the screen. "She tipped you off to a car in Lake Kawayu and indicated you'd find a body in it, but she didn't mention the trunk."

"If she didn't know the body was in the trunk, that rules out Angel as an eyewitness or accomplice, right?"

The corner of Denver's mouth twitched, and she braced herself for sarcasm.

"Maybe, unless Angel saw this at night, knew there was a body somehow, but didn't know where the perpetrator had left it."

No sarcasm detected.

"Yeah, I see how that could happen. Same for an accomplice. She could've left the woman in the car with the killer at the lake and not watched or known what he'd done with the body."

He flicked his finger at the message. "Not much here. You got the message and hightailed it to the lake the next day to look for the car."

"That's how this works. True crime bloggers take a lot on faith. We're not like cops—we don't have to verify, we don't have any rules."

"And that's what gets you in trouble." He brushed his thumb against the mouse. "Angel must've sent you something else to send you on your way to Venice tonight."

She waved her hand in the air. "Keep scrolling. She saw the news and knew I had acted on her tip. She wanted to meet me in person to give me more information. I was supposed to walk along Washington and wait for someone to approach me with a code phrase. That's why I followed the homeless woman—she had the code phrase."

Denver whistled. "Unless Angel is the culprit, somebody learned that code to preempt your meeting."

"I don't think Angel is playing me. Read on. She contacted me after the meeting went south. She thinks someone might be hacking into her computer, and that's how he knew our code phrase."

"That's not good." Denver tapped the keyboard to view the rest of the messages. "Someone reading this knows that Angel tipped you off. Angel put a target on your back…or two targets. Looks like they double-teamed you tonight. One person went to Venice to disrupt the meeting and, while they knew you were out, someone else came here to scribble a warning on your mirror—just in case getting whacked on the head didn't do the trick."

"It didn't." She rubbed the knot on the back of her head.

"Sounds like Angel isn't going to contact you via computer anymore, but that doesn't matter. We have a guy at the station who can track this IP address. We can talk to Angel in person."

"Wait a minute." She pulled the computer from his lap to hers and snapped it shut. "That's not our deal."

"Our deal—" he crunched his soda can in one hand "—is to find the killer of some poor woman stuffed in the trunk of a car."

"My contact is going to help us do it—on her own terms. If she'd wanted to call the cops, she would've done so. If she suspects I'm working with the LAPD, that'll be the end of the flow of information."

"That might be over now."

Denver's cell phone rang and he held up one finger.

"Holt." His dark eyes widened and his fingers tightened on the phone. "Well, isn't that something? I'll pay them a visit first thing tomorrow morning."

The call ended with nothing more than a few grunts on Denver's side. A crease formed between his eyebrows as he tapped the phone against his chin.

The call had something to do with the case…and it was big. She cleared her throat. "I gave you what I had. It's your turn now."

He smacked the phone against his palm, and she jumped. "That car you found in the lake?"

"Yeah?" She twisted her fingers into messy knots.

"It's part of a fleet that belongs to the Campaign to Re-Elect Mayor Wexler."

Chapter Six

The following day, Denver dipped into the parking structure beneath the sleek glass-and-steel structure that housed the offices for the Campaign to Re-Elect Mayor Wexler. Or, as Wexler's staff liked to call it, CREW.

Marino had thrown this case his way, as the detective was busy wrapping up another homicide. Denver was flying solo on this interview, but he had the weight of Chief Sterling behind him. The chief had already given the mayor's office a heads-up—hell, the two men were golfing buddies. As long as their tee time didn't interfere with his investigation, he'd use all the help the chief offered.

Twisting around, Denver grabbed his jacket from the back seat. He'd opted for his most expensive suit for this interview, courtesy of Cool Breeze himself, Detective Billy Crouch. Billy had hooked him up with his personal tailor, and Denver needed as much confidence as he could muster to go charging into the mayor's campaign headquarters asking questions about a dead body in the trunk of one of the campaign's official cars.

He stepped into the elevator, smoothing the lapels of his jacket and using the same motion on the sides of his hair. Either the chief trusted him with this case, or Sterling knew he could manipulate the sap. But this sap had a secret weapon—a redheaded blogger with a burning desire to prove herself.

He'd read some of the stories Ashlynn had written for that magazine she'd worked for, and he had no clue why she was so hell-bent on picking up where her brother had left off. Her brother had a reputation of being anti-police, and the department hadn't been a big fan. Detective Jake McAllister had only agreed to work with Sean Hughes because the guy had opened a channel of communication with one of The Player's copycats. But in the end, Hughes had gotten burned by that fire when The Player himself had killed him for interference.

He hoped like hell Ashlynn wasn't traveling down the same path as her brother. He hoped like hell he wasn't leading her down that path.

The elevator dinged on the ninth floor of the building, and Denver gave his tie a tug and exited onto a slick tiled floor. He swiveled his head in search of a reception desk or receptionist, but the floorplan stretched into a large, light open space with cubbies here and there, exercise balls in front of desks in lieu of chairs and a few glass-walled offices hugging the perimeter of the room.

As his gaze tracked among the busy worker bees,

he cleared his throat. Not one of them looked up or even broke stride. If nobody was going to play nice, he'd be as intrusive as possible.

Making a beeline for one of those offices, he squared his shoulders and plunged into the melee, skirting desks and charging past the exercise balls, sending them skittering sideways. That earned him a few quick glances and openmouthed stares.

Out of the corner of his eye, he saw a man scurrying toward him, a laptop clutched to his chest. "Excuse me. Excuse me, Detective Holt?"

Ah, so they *were* expecting him. Denver halted in midstride and swung around on the guy, causing him to stumble to a stop. A second minion careened through the desks to intercept them, her oversized glasses giving her a startled, bug-eyed look—or maybe she was startled.

Denver stuck out his hand to the man with the laptop. "Detective Denver Holt. You must be Christian Bushnell."

Bushnell juggled the laptop in his arms and shook Denver's hand, his mouth twisting up at the corner as Denver went in for the hard squeeze. "Nice to meet you, Detective Holt. This is my coworker, Amalia Fernandez."

Denver finally released Bushnell's hand and turned to Amalia, who was much better at navigating the handshake and the laptop, which was tucked under her left arm.

Did these people walk around with laptops and tablets attached to their bodies?

"Good morning, Detective Holt. I'm the mayor's campaign director and Christian is my assistant." She sure wanted to set the record straight. She swept an arm to the side. "We'll be talking in one of the offices for privacy."

"Looks like that's in short supply here."

Amalia drew back her shoulders and flicked her neat dark ponytail. "Mayor Wexler prides himself on transparency."

Always campaigning, this bunch. Must be exhausting. Denver gave a tight smile. "That's what I'm counting on."

He followed the two of them to an office with glass walls that looked out onto the controlled chaos of the rest of the room. If the Northwest Division had interview rooms like these, the cops wouldn't garner half the confessions they got.

He pulled out the chair Amalia indicated with a nod of her head and tried to perch on the edge. The slant and cushioning of the seat made that difficult. The cops would have even more trouble getting confessions out of anyone sitting in these chairs.

He grabbed the edge of the table to keep from sliding back into the black leather, and plucked a notebook from the front pocket of his shirt. He smacked it on the table, and Amalia and Christian both flinched.

Not as calm and collected as they appeared.

"You both know why I'm here. A body was found in the trunk of a car that belongs to this office, and the car was sitting at the bottom of Lake Kawayu."

Christian shook his head. "I had no idea that lake was so deep."

Amalia shot him a look and may have even kicked him under the table because Christian clamped his mouth shut and reddened up to his eyeballs.

"I—I mean, we were shocked when we found out."

"We heard the news, Detective Holt." Amalia folded her hands in her lap. "We, and that includes the mayor, were so distressed. What can we do to help? Mayor Wexler has instructed us to cooperate fully, of course, and has assured his good friend, Chief Sterling, that we're here to help."

"That's good to know." Denver held his pen poised above a clean sheet on his notepad. "Why did you tamper with the license plate and VIN on that car?"

Christian swallowed a big lump in his throat and Amalia's smile froze on her face. "Excuse me. We don't tamper with license plates or destroy the VINs on our cars, and didn't do so to that car. Whoever stole the car from our garage must've done that."

"That car was stolen?"

"Of course." Amalia spread her hands on the table. "This is LA, Detective, the car theft capital of the world."

Denver opened his eyes wide. "Even with Mayor Wexler at the helm?"

The smile stayed plastered on Amalia's lipsticked mouth, but had dropped completely from her eyes.

"One of the many issues he's going to address in his second term."

Hunching forward, Denver placed the tip of his pen on the paper in front of him. "When did you report the car stolen?"

"We didn't." Amalia pursed her lips and jutted her chin out aggressively.

He knew they hadn't reported it stolen, and she knew he knew. He let his pen drop to the table, and Christian's reaction would've made you think he'd fired a shot instead of dropped a pen.

Denver screwed up his face. "Oh, I'm sorry. I misunderstood. I thought you said the car had been stolen from your lot."

Crossing her arms, Amalia said, "You didn't misunderstand, Detective Holt. You knew we hadn't reported it stolen, or you would've already had that report in your hand. We have a lot of cars in our fleet here at CREW. We don't always keep track of them as well as we should. We didn't notice this car was gone, but I can assure you, somebody stole that car out of our garage."

"You might've just solved the crime, Ms. Fernandez. You have cameras at the garage?" He scribbled some gibberish in his notebook. They were both too far away to read it anyway.

"We do have cameras, and I'm a step ahead of you, Detective. I've already ordered the security footage. Unfortunately, we keep it for seven days only, so if the car was stolen before that…" Amalia shrugged her shoulders.

Denver mumbled under his breath. "That's convenient."

"Excuse me?" Amalia narrowed her eyes.

"I said, how inconvenient, but we'll work with what we have." He rapped on the desk just because he liked seeing Christian jump. "I'm going to need a list of everyone who works on the campaign."

"What?" Christian had finally found his voice, and it had a decided squeak that had been missing before. "We have hundreds of people working on CREW."

"I hope you can print out all those names from a database. That'll make it easy." Denver snapped his fingers. "I'll do you one better. Get me the list of people who worked on the campaign *and* had access to the fleet of vehicles. I'll take that breakdown first, and then you can supply the names of all the campaign workers."

Amalia drummed a sharp set of talons on the table. "Waste of time, Detective Holt. I already told you the car was stolen."

She'd gone too far even for Christian, who shot her a worried look from beneath a creased brow.

Denver clapped a hand over his heart. "Thanks for your concern and, uh, expertise, Ms. Fernandez, but you let me worry about what's a waste of time and what's not." He picked up his pen again. "What do staffers use the cars for?"

To make up for Amalia's misstep, Christian launched in helpfully. "All sorts of things—delivering items to campaign stops, doing door-to-doors, providing transportation for the mayor's guests for speeches and events, e-even picking up lunch for the CREW."

"Do all these perks come from the city budget?"

Christian opened his mouth but Amalia cut him off with a slicing motion. "Absolutely not. That would be a campaign violation. The cars, the lunches, everything you see here is funded by the Campaign to Re-Elect Mayor Wexler."

Denver held up his hands in surrender. "Hey, sounds good to me. I'm here to investigate a homicide, not the mayor's finances."

Sitting perpendicular to the office door, Denver spotted a man in a cap with the parking service logo on the front approaching the office.

Amalia jumped up before the guy finished knocking. "Thank you, Gerardo."

She took something from his hand and started to close the door, but Denver pushed back his chair and lunged forward, putting his foot against the doorjamb. "Gerardo, can I ask you a couple of questions? I'm Detective Holt with the LAPD."

Gerardo slid a glance to Amalia before saying, "Yes, sir."

Denver pointed to the thumb drive swinging from a ribbon wrapped around Amalia's index finger. "That contains the footage from the garage for the past seven days?"

"Yes, it does. It covers both exits, so it catches any cars that left the parking garage by either exit in the last week."

"No way to get footage from more than seven days ago."

"I'm afraid not, Detective. It's taped over."

Denver felt in his front pocket and pulled out a card. He extended it to Gerardo. "Call me if you remember anything about the cars in Mayor Wexler's fleet, or anything unusual in the garage the past few weeks."

"I'll do that." Gerardo murmured something in Spanish to Amalia, and she gave a quick shake of her head.

Denver didn't know if he would've understood it even if he spoke fluent Spanish—which he didn't.

When Amalia closed the door after Gerardo, she dangled the thumb drive in front of Denver. "Here you go, Detective. I thought it would be easier for you to review the footage at the station. If you have any questions about it, you can call Gerardo."

He pocketed the thumb drive. "Thanks, Ms. Fernandez. Did, uh, Gerardo have something to add at the end there?"

She blinked her eyes, rapidly. "He just asked if he could use the restroom here on his way out."

"Oh, you didn't let him?"

She opened her mouth once and snapped it closed.

"I mean, you shook your head like no."

"We don't allow anyone but staffers to use the restrooms on this floor." She gave him a tight smile. "I think Gerardo understood. Now, is there anything else, Detective Holt?"

"One more thing." He held up a finger. "Do either of you know the name Tiana Fuller?"

Denver shifted his gaze to Christian, the weak link. The boy didn't disappoint. Christian's Adam's apple bobbed as if he'd just swallowed a golf ball.

Amalia didn't give Christian the chance to step in it, though. "Never heard that name before. Is she the…victim? A suspect?"

"Can't say right now." He tipped his head toward Christian. "You?"

"Wh-what?" The color rushed from Christian's throat to his cheeks. He'd never make it as a poker player.

"Have you ever heard the name Tiana Fuller or know who she is?"

Christian rolled his eyes to the ceiling. If he'd had a thinking cap, he'd have slapped it on his head. "No. No, I haven't."

"That's all I have—for now." He tapped his finger next to the card Amalia had left on the desk. "Give me a call if you think of anything else. I'll review the footage from the garage while waiting for you to send over the list of campaign workers. I expect that today, right?"

"Of course. I'll have Christian get right on that for you. Shouldn't take long." Amalia opened the door. "Mayor Wexler is anxious to clear this up, and his office will be sending condolences to the family— once we know the identity of the victim. Will you let us know, Detective Holt, or do we find out from the TV news like everyone else?"

"I'll let you know as soon as we get an ID—just in case."

"In case?" She narrowed her dark eyes.

"In case she's connected to the campaign...or Mayor Wexler."

Chapter Seven

After he'd mentioned Tiana's name in connection to Mayor Wexler, Amalia escorted him out of the CREW office so fast he could hear the wind whistling past his ears. When he reached his car, he shrugged out of his jacket and smoothed it out carefully in the back seat.

He'd like to get Christian alone, but Amalia had probably already schooled him in the proper responses to this investigation—we know nothing, the mayor knows nothing.

Denver checked his phone and his heart pounded as he listened to a voice mail from Captain Fields. Mrs. Edmunds had delivered her daughter's DNA to the station, and if he hurried, he might be back in time to learn whether or not Tiana Fuller was their victim.

He positioned his phone on the console for the Bluetooth and tamped down the disappointment he felt over the absence of a message from Ashlynn. Maybe she didn't want to step on his toes and ex-

pected him to take the lead. They had a business relationship, not a romantic one.

He tapped in her number and her phone rang
through the speakers. She answered after the second ring, out of breath, as if she'd just jogged a mile
or two.

Before he could even get through the niceties, she
asked, "Did you read the blog post?"

"I did. It was good. You're a good writer."

She coughed. "Does that mean it grabbed you by
the throat and left you wanting more?"

She left him wanting more.

He cranked up the AC. "Yeah, it was like a story,
a mystery. Have you gotten any more tips? Hear from
Angel?"

"I've gotten tons of public comments, and a few
weird private ones that I'm still sorting through."
She paused, taking a sip of something. "Do you have
anything for me yet? Has she been ID'd?"

"Not yet. We're working on it." Denver glanced
in his rearview and accelerated onto the freeway.
"Weird tips? Do you feel safe?"

"Yeah. I had a locksmith come out and install
a proper lock on the sliding door and got the glass
replaced. I'm submitting everything to my insurance company. I mean renter's insurance has to cover
something, right?"

At her breezy tone, he loosened his grip on the
steering wheel. He hadn't cared about anyone's safety
for a long time. He'd made sure he never cared about
anyone enough to worry about them. After his fa-

ther's murder, he'd driven himself, and everyone around him, crazy with his hovering and double-checking. Had given himself an ulcer, too—at least, that's what the department-mandated shrink, Kyra Chase, had told him.

He licked his lips. "Wouldn't hurt to get a security system, maybe a camera. Lots of people have them these days."

"I'll look into it. If that lipstick message and the assault at Venice Beach meant to warn me off, I'm not heeding it. Who knows what this person will try next?"

Denver's palms broke out in a sweat and he wiped them, one by one, on his slacks.

He needed to back off. If she wanted to put herself in danger, that was her business. He had a job protecting people—strangers. Mom had a new husband, and his sister had married a guy with hundreds of relatives practically living on top of them. He'd relinquished the reins of their protection to others, and he had no intention of picking up another set. "Okay, keep me posted, and let me know if you hear from Angel again. I'll tell you what I can."

He ended the call abruptly and sped back to the station.

When he got there, he bypassed his new desk in Robbery-Homicide and went straight to the lab. The remodel of the Northeast Division had included a state-of-the-art lab where the techs could do DNA matching.

He sidled up next to Lori Del Valle, one of the fingerprint techs. "DNA match done yet?"

"No, it isn't." She shoved at his arm. "Watching the techs isn't going to make it go any faster, but nobody has located Tiana Fuller yet."

He sucked in his lower lip. "It's not looking too good for Tiana. Her mother tentatively identified the top our victim was wearing as Tiana's."

"We know you're lead on this case, Denver. We're going to tell you first." The nudge at his arm turned into a pat.

"Too eager, huh?"

"Understandable." She tossed him a baggie. "But, hey, I processed the tube of lipstick and there are no prints at all—none. That means it was probably wiped."

"I figured." He put his finger to his lips. "Just between us, right?"

"Discretion is my middle name."

"Don't wanna get you in trouble again." He meandered back to the Robbery-Homicide room with a little less spring in his step and dropped his bag next to his desk.

Detective Falco nodded as she walked past him. "How'd it go at the mayor's re-election office?"

"As you'd expect—closemouthed groupies doing their best to protect their guy."

"You know the chief's going to want you to back off as soon as the CREW is cleared of any association with this woman."

"I'm aware, and I plan to back off when no more arrows point in that direction."

"Good answer."

When she dove to answer a phone, Denver inserted the thumb drive from the garage into his computer. Detective Falco obviously didn't envy him this assignment. The chief could've assigned this to the golden boys—McAllister and Crouch—but there's no way he could control those two. Could the chief control him? Denver could think of a few ways Sterling might try.

He queued up the footage to the very first minute that was available and hunched forward to watch the flickering images on his monitor. He had the gate to Santa Monica Boulevard on the top of his screen, and the one to the side street on the bottom. Seemed like most of the CREW's cars used the side street. The sedans all looked the same, and he kept his eyes on the license plates. Although the plates on the car in the lake had been swapped, he knew the real plate number from the VIN and doubted someone had spent time in the garage removing the plates before driving it out of the garage. And if someone had done that? He'd locate the car without the plates.

When he made it through day one without a hit, he snatched a bag of chips from his desk drawer and popped it open. He rubbed his eyes, and then stuffed several chips in his mouth, crunching as he watched the first car of the next day roll under the parking arm.

He jumped when someone clamped his shoulder. "Boy does not live by chips alone. That footage isn't going anywhere while you get some lunch."

Denver twisted his head around, glancing at Billy's

smiling face. Easy for him to say. "One day down, six to go."

"My guess?" Billy circled his finger in the air over the monitor. "You're not going to see that car on camera. The person who took it had to know that it was going to be ID'd sooner or later, even without the correct plates, registration and a scratched-up VIN. He either knew about the footage being taped over every week, or he did something to the cameras."

Denver clicked the mouse to stop the footage and licked salt from his lips. "Tell me something, Cool Breeze. How come you and McAllister aren't on this case? A murder of a young woman, found in a public place, in a car belonging to the Campaign to Re-Elect Mayor Wexler? Sounds right up the alley of the dynamic duo."

Billy brushed his knuckles down his tie, as if worried some of the salt from Denver's chips had attached themselves to the silk. "If you don't know the answer to that, my man, you're probably never going to make permanent detective in Robbery-Homicide."

Denver nodded. The chief couldn't pressure J-Mac and Crouch like he could the new guy. Denver crumpled a napkin in his left hand. "Any advice?"

"Just do your job, Rocky."

"Rocky?" Denver lifted an eyebrow. Like all squads in the LAPD, Robbery-Homicide was notorious for assigning nicknames to the detectives.

"You know—Denver? Rocky Mountain High?"

Denver groaned and shot the balled-up napkin at the sharp crease in Billy's impeccable slacks.

He spent the next two hours speeding through the remaining days, too. As he watched the last car on the footage roll beneath the parking arm, he slumped in his chair. Billy had nailed it. The killer hadn't made this easy. He'd either taken the car in advance, without reporting it, or he'd tampered with the camera or footage. Denver had been watching the counter on the footage and hadn't noticed anything hinky.

Someone had taken the car in advance of the murder—either planning the murder or planning something else he or she hadn't wanted tracked. Or maybe it was dumb luck. Someone took the car without planning anything at all.

Denver pinched the bridge of his nose as his stomach rumbled. A bag of potato chips didn't cut it for lunch.

His desk phone rang and he grabbed it. "Holt."

Lance from the lab said, "We have the DNA match to Tiana Fuller. She is the victim in the trunk of the car."

"Thanks, Lance." Denver's eye twitched.

The ID of a victim always cut both ways. Knowing the victim allowed the investigation to progress in a valuable way, but it also meant ripping apart another family. He'd personally notify Mrs. Edmunds. In most of the homicide investigations he'd worked, he'd become the go-to guy for family notifications, given his own background.

He almost felt it his duty to take on the notifications to protect the other detectives from sinking into the grief pit with the families. He'd already visited that pit, had already been scarred by it.

Taking a deep breath, he swiveled his chair toward the wall and stared at a spot near the ceiling. Then he called Mrs. Edmonds.

She answered after the first ring. She'd been waiting for his call. "Hello? Detective Holt?"

"It is, Mrs. Edmonds. We identified the victim in the trunk of the submerged car as your daughter, Tiana. There is no doubt. The DNA matches the sample you submitted." He held his breath.

Other cops might dance around, might try to couch the news in soft, pretty words. The families of victims didn't want or need that.

Mrs. Edmonds let out a sob. "I knew it."

His chest tightened, and he loosened his collar. "I'm sorry for your loss. I'm going to need to talk to you and your husband. Get a list of Tiana's friends, boyfriends, roommates—but not now. Tomorrow okay?"

She sniffled. "Tomorrow is fine, Detective."

She ended the call before he could respond, but he really had no response. There were no words, and sometimes words made it all worse.

He studied the spot on the wall and flicked the pad of his thumb beneath his eye. Then he spun his chair back to his computer. The garage footage had held his attention all afternoon, although from the corner of his eye he could see emails popping up every so often at the bottom of his screen. Now, he scanned through them, the last of the bunch from Lance with the DNA report, and cursed under his breath.

Christian at the CREW had failed to send the database of campaign workers. As he grabbed his jacket, he tapped Christian's number on his phone. He left the guy a not-so-civil voice mail reminding him what he owed him.

After he left the message, he listened to one from Ashlynn on his way out of the station, inviting him for dinner tonight. Probably wanted to pick his brain some more, find out if he'd learned the identity of the victim.

He'd promised to play ball with her and, as long as Tiana's family knew first, he didn't have a problem releasing Tiana's name to Ashlynn. Her identity would be all over the news and social media by tomorrow morning anyway.

And his rumbling stomach told him the invitation couldn't have come at a better time. He texted her Tiana's name and accepted the invite to dinner, asking if she wanted him to bring anything. Picked brain or no, he never went to anyone's house empty-handed.

A half hour later, as the freeway spit him out onto one of the boulevards bordering Culver City, he stooped over his steering wheel, looking for a liquor store. Ashlynn had promised stir-fried beef and veggies, so he picked up a Pinot Grigio. He also grabbed a bag of trail mix just in case he had to wait for dinner.

He pulled up to the curb across the street from her duplex, opened his door and dusted the salt from the peanuts from his hands and slacks. He still had on his good suit and didn't want to spoil the effect. To top it off, he reached for his jacket in the back seat and slid his arms into the sleeves. Might as well maintain the appearance of a business meeting—with stir-fry.

He knocked on her door, and he heard a chain slide and a dead bolt click. When she opened it, he said, "I'm glad to hear you're taking your security seriously."

She stepped back to let him over the threshold. "When the guy from the lock and key shop came out to install the contraption on the sliding door, I asked him to install a new dead bolt and a chain—just in case."

He sniffed the air and while the smell of ginger didn't do anything for him, he knew it heralded more savory tastes. He held up the bottle in the bag. "Pinot Grigio?"

"Sounds good." She took the bag from him and peeked inside. "Is it cold by any chance?"

"No, sorry. The liquor store had only the cheap stuff refrigerated."

"That's okay. I'll stick it in the freezer and it should at least be chilled by the time we eat."

He nodded, grateful for the trail mix rattling around in his empty stomach. "Have you already released the news about Tiana Fuller on your blog?"

"I have, thanks." She sidestepped into the kitchen and ducked into the refrigerator. "Terrible news for her family."

He clasped the back of his neck. "Yeah, it was."

Waving a hand over his clothes, she said, "Straight from work. I'll take your jacket, and you can lose the tie. You can even lose the shoes, if you like."

"I can just hang it over a chair." He shrugged out of the jacket and made a move toward a kitchen chair pulled up to the small table, already set for two.

She snatched it from him and held it up, giving it the once-over. "It looks expensive. I used to write about fashion. I know, it's hard to believe."

"It's my one really good suit." His gaze swept across her skinny jeans that hit right above her ankles, a pair of gleaming white tennis shoes and light green top that dipped into a V on her chest. She'd swept her red hair into a half up, half down ponytail. She looked neat and crisp, and good enough to eat.

He swallowed. Man, he really was hungry.

She rested her cheek against the material of his jacket and ran one hand down the sleeve. The gesture twisted his stomach into knots. He had a hunger for more than just food.

"It's nice. I'll hang it up." She crossed back over to the hallway and opened a door to the closet. "Don't forget it."

"Do you need some help?" He jerked his thumb at the wok on the counter, next to a cutting board filled with a colorful array of veggies.

She snapped her fingers. "You can warm up the lumpia and eat it."

"Lumpia?" His mouth instantly watered.

"I know I'm sort of crossing cultures here, but my friend Mercy made the lumpia and dropped some off today. It's in the fridge and just needs some heat. Microwave will do."

He opened the fridge and slid a plastic container

from the shelf. He popped the lid. "Homemade and everything, huh? My buddy's mom was from the Philippines and always whipped up homemade lumpia when I went to his house. My favorite deep-fried snack. Looked just like this."

She pointed to the microwave. "Not too long. Maybe a minute. You can start eating that while I'm cooking this."

As he put the container in the microwave, Ashlynn peeled the foil from a bowl of beef strips, marinating in some sauce that made his eyes sting. "You were planning this dinner for a while?"

She cranked up the heat under the wok, and her cheeks sported two red spots. "I was planning to cook this for myself tonight after Mercy dropped off the lumpia. Some of us single people still eat more than takeout and pizza."

"We do?" The microwave beeped and he punched the button with his knuckle to open the door. "I know every pizza delivery place within a five-mile radius of my place in the Marina."

"You live in Marina del Rey? Apartment?"

"Condo."

"Must be nice." She jumped back as the meat sizzled and popped in the pan. "I figured you might live closer to the police station up north."

He'd bought the condo with the proceeds from his dad's rental property in Oregon. Dad had left that property to him and his sister, with his mom's blessing.

"I, uh—" he carefully removed the container

from the microwave with the tips of his fingers and dropped it on the counter "—used to work Pacific Division. Transferred to Northeast a few years ago for Vice. The commute's not that bad."

"I have chopsticks on the table, and Mercy included some spicy red chili sauce for dipping. Why don't you dig in while I finish this?" She prodded the vegetables in the wok and they hissed back at her.

She didn't have to tell him twice. He backed up to the table, grabbed a pair of chopsticks and fished the red sauce from the fridge. He maneuvered a piece of lumpia between his chopsticks and dipped it into the sauce. He closed his eyes while he chewed.

Ashlynn laughed and nudged him with her elbow. "That good, huh?"

"It would be nirvana even if I weren't starving."

"I knew it. You had that rangy, feral look about you." She puffed a lock of hair from her face. "You wanna give me one of those? I'm a little busy here."

He plucked up another lumpia, dunked it in the sauce, and held it out toward her puckered lips, almost as red as the sauce. She took the snack with her teeth and sucked it into her mouth.

Rolling her eyes at the ceiling, she said, "Yummy."

He devoured two more while she finished the stir-fry and the rice cooker clicked off.

Ashlynn grabbed two plates, piled both high with sticky white rice, and ladled the beef and veggies on top. "There's more, if you want seconds."

"I probably will." He brought the wine and the lumpia to the table while she set down the plates.

She collapsed in a chair and then hopped up again. "A corkscrew would be nice—I mean, since you said it wasn't the cheap stuff. The bottle probably doesn't have a screw top."

"It does not." He took the corkscrew from her and did the honors. "Only slightly chilled."

She held the glass to her lips and the reflection of the wine rippled in her eyes as she gazed at him over the edge. "You seem more…human tonight."

He took a swig of the wine and felt the warmth flow through his veins. "I had to tell Mrs. Edmonds today that we'd ID'd Tiana as the body in the vehicle. That kind of conversation tends to awaken your humanity, no matter how far you've buried it."

She cocked her head and ran a finger around the rim of her glass where she'd left a sticky print from her lips. "Why is yours buried?"

He concentrated on scooping up some rice and meat with his chopsticks. "What's the internet saying about Tiana? I'm sure you've already taken a peek in between marinating meat and chopping veggies."

She blinked at his abrupt change of subject and tapped the side of her plate with her chopsticks. "Just the usual speculation—sex worker, trafficking, drugs, online dating gone wrong. Nobody knows about the car yet."

"I'm glad you didn't release that information on your blog. I'm sure it'll get out soon enough, though. Everyone at CREW must know it now, and everyone in parking services at that building."

She raised her eyebrows. "You told me not to release it. I'm still trying to gain your trust, here. It seems like an important detail to withhold, doesn't it? I may be just a blogger, but I have my protocols, as well. If you spew out too much information, you can't discern the crackpots from the people who really know something."

"That's exactly how *we* operate. I figured the more crackpots, the better for you."

She crossed her chopsticks on the edge of her plate. "We really do want to help, you know. It's not all about the clicks. My brother's proudest moments as a true crime blogger were when he actually got to help an investigation."

"Like he thought he was doing with The Player."

"Exactly, even though it cost him his life."

He toyed with a grain of rice on his plate. "That guy I talked to at the mayor's campaign office was supposed to send me a list of campaign workers, highlighting the ones who had access to the vehicles."

"He didn't do it?" She widened her blue eyes, and the smattering of freckles stood out on her nose.

"Nope. I left him a strongly worded voice mail. Now, I'm wondering if they're cleansing the records."

"To protect their own? Why would they want to protect a killer?"

He shrugged. "Their job is to re-elect Wexler. They don't want him to look bad."

"Once it becomes common knowledge that a CREW campaign car is connected to Tiana's death, it's not gonna help. They'll have to go into ultra-spin mode."

"I think they're in that mode right now. Maybe Tiana even worked for the campaign. She was old enough to vote." He dangled a piece of meat over his plate. "This is really good, by the way."

"Thanks. I'm glad you accepted my invitation, though I have a feeling you did so because I caught you at the right moment. No time for lunch today?"

"Busted." He stuffed the meat into his mouth.

They, or rather he, finished the rest of the food, and he washed it down with another half glass of wine. He poured her another glass and volunteered to clean up the kitchen.

As he rinsed the plates at the sink, Ashlynn settled on the couch with her laptop. He said, "I'm assuming you didn't get anything from Angel since I talked to you today."

"Angel has been mum." The keyboard clicked as her fingers raced across it. "Denver?"

"Yeah?" The tone of her voice caused a dish to slip through his soapy fingers and fall into the sink with a clatter. "Angel?"

"I don't think so, but an important bit of evidence just the same—if it can be believed."

He shut off the water. "What is it?"

"You're not going to find Tiana on the rolls of the campaign workers for Wexler."

"Why is that?"

"Because she worked for his opposition—the Campaign to Elect Veronica Escalante."

Chapter Eight

Ashlynn watched Denver through narrowed eyes, not moving a muscle, her hand hovering over the keyboard. Would he discount her information? Ridicule her sources?

He turned from the sink and wiped his hands on the dishtowel, his eyebrows creating a vee between his eyes. "You're sure it's not from Angel?"

"Funny how you trust Angel all of a sudden. This is from my blog post where I released Tiana's name. It's among the responses." She squinted at the screen. "It already has over a hundred up-votes and a few theories attached to it."

He balled up the towel in his hands and tossed it onto the counter. "Theories but not corroborating proof. Who is this person who posted the link between Tiana and Escalante's campaign?"

"You really wanna know?" She wedged the soles of her sneakers against the edge of the coffee table and expelled a breath. "It was Lil' Snoop."

Denver snorted and cranked on the water to finish

the dishes. "We're supposed to believe a statement from someone called Lil' Snoop?"

"It's more than anything coming from someone called LAPD Detective."

"Ouch."

"Think about it, Denver. The LAPD didn't release the information that the car in the lake belonged to the CREW. That's a hell of a coincidence that Lil' Snoop knows Tiana worked for the opposition campaign without knowing she was found in a CREW car."

He retrieved the dishtowel and carefully dried the wok as if it were made of priceless crystal. "The LAPD didn't release that information, but like I said, someone else could have."

Ashlynn's blood boiled and she smacked her palm against her chest. "Me? Is that what you're saying? You think I released that info?"

He waved the dishtowel like a white flag. "I didn't say that."

"You didn't have to. I got the message." She shoved off the couch, clutching the sides of her laptop. "Do you want to see? You read my blog today. I didn't mention the connection to Mayor Wexler."

"I believe you, but there are others who knew. The CREW knew—at least, Amalia and Christian."

"You said they wanted to hush it up. That's not something they're going to voluntarily release." She perched on the arm of her couch, balancing her laptop on her knees, her temper cooling. "Even if that information did get out, it doesn't mean Lil' Snoop is wrong."

"Okay, what cred does this…Snoop have? Is he or she a regular poster on the blog?" Denver shook out the towel and hung it over the oven door handle.

"He is a regular poster and seems to have inside information. He won't tell us his profession, but he has connections in the city. He's usually right. He posts publicly, but he's never messaged me privately." She slid onto a cushion of the couch and crooked her finger at Denver. "Come here. I'll show you how it looks, and you can read the theories with me."

He joined her on the couch, the sleeves of his dress shirt rolled up, exposing strong forearms corded with veins and muscle. He looked as if he were capable of doing a lot more than the dishes.

He hunched over her shoulder, smelling of dish soap and hot chilies. "Okay, let me see what Snoop has."

She scooted the laptop closer to his legs and jabbed a finger at the screen. "This is his first post—a comment to my blog update naming the victim as Tiana Fuller."

Denver's shoulder pressed against hers as he bent forward for a closer look. "He made that comment less than an hour after your post. That's fast work. I'm still waiting to get the list of names from the CREW."

"Looks legit, right? He doesn't mention the car from Wexler's campaign because he doesn't know about it."

Denver rubbed his knuckles across his sexy stubble. "If this guy's so plugged in, why doesn't he know about the car?"

"That's the beauty of the citizen sleuth." She drew a circle in the air over the screen. "It's small pieces coming together. One person knows one thing. Someone else knows something else. There are people from all walks of life chiming in."

"What I want to know is why these people aren't coming to the police. Why didn't this Lil' Whoever call the LAPD with this information?" He sat back against the couch and shoved a hand through his dark hair.

"There are lots of reasons, Denver. In Lil' Snoop's case, it could be that he'd get in trouble for releasing information. Some people don't want to go on record. Some people don't want the cops sniffing around."

"Great." He slumped, kicking out one leg, resting his shoe on her coffee table. "I'm going to have to make a visit to the Escalante campaign tomorrow to check this out, after I talk to Tiana's parents. I need to get a list of her friends, boyfriends, her phone carrier—that is, unless you can get all that from your blog."

"Silly." She slugged his hard bicep. "Even I know this stuff isn't admissible evidence for a search warrant."

He raised an eyebrow. "Ever hear of anonymous sources? I'm not going to serve a search warrant on Councilwoman Escalante's campaign headquarters, anyway. I'll just drop by for a friendly visit."

"Weird, isn't it?"

"That Tiana worked for one campaign and was found dead in the car of another? Yeah, weird." He tipped his head toward the computer. "What's the theory online?"

"That someone from Wexler's campaign murdered her to make Escalante look bad."

"And stuffed her in a Wexler car? How's that gonna work out for them?"

"The posters don't know she was found in a CREW car, though, do they?"

"But we do." Denver chewed on his bottom lip, his dark eyes unreadable.

Did the *we* mean him and her, or the LAPD?

She asked, "Do you have a theory of your own?"

"Not yet. I want to talk to her parents first. I want to get to know Tiana."

"Sadly, it's too late for that." Her bottom lip trembled as she thought about that poor young woman in the trunk of the car.

Denver sat up sharply. "I can't save her now, but I can find her killer and get her and her family some justice. That's the thing with being a homicide detective. We come in after the damage has already been done. We're not expected to save anyone, except by getting a killer off the streets."

His vehemence had startled her, as if he were defending his role in the criminal justice process.

"That's huge. You are saving countless, nameless, faceless others by tracking down a killer. Look at The Player copycats. Each time the task force apprehended one of the copycats, it saved the lives of others in their murderous paths."

"That's the idea. Even if Tiana's killer has no intention of striking again, he needs to be brought to justice. I'll get him."

His jaw hardened, and she believed him. She just hoped he'd let her help.

THE FOLLOWING MORNING, Ashlynn rolled onto her side and opened one eye. She stretched her arm across the other side of the bed and smoothed her hand over the undisturbed bedspread. She slept in a king-sized bed, but she barely moved in her sleep. Making the bed consisted of flipping up the covers and tucking in the side of the sheet.

It had been a long time since someone had messed up that other side of the bed. Her ex-boyfriend had been a cheater, and she hadn't felt like venturing into the dating world since. Then Sean had been murdered, and dating had slipped further down her list of priorities.

Her hand bunched the smooth sheets next to her. Didn't mean she didn't miss a body next to hers— especially a body like Detective Denver Holt's.

Despite the sexual tension between them last night, Denver had kept things professional. Or maybe the tension was hers alone.

Sighing, she scooted from the bed and flicked up the corner. Before she even hit the bathroom, she pulled her laptop onto the bed and accessed her blog.

People had gone crazy over the "The Girl in the

Lake" story. Her scoop on the victim's name last night had resulted in an overload of comments. The LAPD had sent a news release to the mainstream media, and Tiana's name and picture were all over the internet now...but she'd been first with it.

She owed Denver, big-time, and she had to deliver more than dinner if she hoped to keep the flow of information coming. She sent a private message to Angel, asking if she was okay and if she'd known Tiana. Ashlynn didn't expect a response, but she wanted Angel to know she still trusted her even after the debacle in Venice.

One idea of how she could help Denver had come to her as she'd drifted off to sleep last night. The plan looked even better in the light of day, and she'd put it into action as soon as she could.

She showered and dressed young—jeans, T-shirt, tennis shoes—pretty much how she usually dressed, leaving off the makeup and scooping her hair into a high ponytail. The sun had come through early this morning, and one of those warm, So Cal spring days called out to everyone to abandon the office and stick their toes in the sand.

Her office didn't resemble most nine-to-five joints, but she couldn't ditch work anyway.

As she nibbled on the edge of a piece of toast spread with crunchy peanut butter, her cell phone buzzed. She wiped her fingers on a napkin and studied the display. Sean always said unknown numbers were the best kind.

She answered with a cautious note to her voice. "Hello?"

"Ashlynn Hughes?" The woman on the line didn't wait for confirmation before launching ahead. "This is Megan Wright with KTOP. Your blog, *LA Confidential*, published Tiana Fuller's name as the victim in the submerged car in Lake Kawayu before the LAPD released its news item to the press. How did you get that information?"

Ashlynn swallowed. As a news reporter, Megan should know all about confidential sources, and Detective Denver Holt was the most confidential source she'd ever had.

She took a small sip of orange juice. "Hi, Megan. I have my sources, just like you do, and they are every bit as confidential. I'm not at liberty to release the name of my source."

"Got a live one, huh?" Megan chuckled. "Good for you. I, and everyone else, am going to be keeping my eye on the blog. You also found the body. Did that come from this source, as well?"

"No comment." Ashlynn dabbed at a few crumbs on her plate and sucked them into her mouth.

"Are the cops all over you on this yet?"

"No comment."

"Okay, okay. Just keep me in mind for…anything." Megan coughed and lowered her voice. "And I want to tell you how sorry I was about Sean's death. I almost feel responsible."

Ashlynn's hand moved up to her throat. "You?

How? The Player killed Sean for working with one of his copycats."

"I knew your brother, had collaborated with him on a few things. I'm the one who suggested his blog as a means of communication between the copycat killer and Detective McAllister." The polished reporter sucked in a breath and her voice wavered. "I wish I had never done it."

"Don't blame yourself. Sean would've killed for that opportunity. You knew that, and gave it to him. Instead, *he* got killed, but you couldn't have predicted that. Nobody could."

She sniffed. "Just know I considered your brother a friend, and if there's anything I can do for you, just ask."

Sounded like she could do a lot more for Megan than the reporter could do for her. "I'll keep it in mind, and thanks for your condolences."

Ashlynn dumped her plate in the sink, checked her locks and grabbed her keys.

Wouldn't Megan Wright like to know where she was headed right now? Wouldn't Detective Denver Holt? She had no intention of telling either one.

Forty-five minutes later, she breezed through the double glass doors of Veronica Escalante's campaign headquarters. She surveyed the room, bustling with phones and computer activity, but that lasted only a few seconds as a man emerged from one of the offices with a view of the room. He barreled toward her, a used-car-salesman smile on his lips and suspicious beady eyes drilling into her.

"Can I help you?"

She cocked her head, her ponytail swinging behind her. "I hope I can help you. I'm Jenny Cochrane. I'm a poli-sci major at UCLA, and I'd love to volunteer for Councilwoman Escalante's campaign for mayor."

"Excellent. I'm Jed Gordon, Veronica's campaign manager." He snapped his fingers in the air. "You can fill out a form with a few details about yourself, and we'll put you to work."

"Sweet." Ashlynn clasped her hands in front of her. "I have some time now before my classes start. Is there something I can help out with?"

Jed's snaps had produced a decidedly less enthusiastic campaign volunteer, who shuffled toward them, brushing long, black hair from her face and pouting with a pair of collagen-injected lips.

Jed spared the volunteer a quick glance and said, "How are your envelope-stuffing skills?"

Ashlynn held her hands up and wiggled her fingers. "Top-notch."

The dark-haired woman snickered and asked, "What do you want?"

Jed's lips stretched into a smile. "Lulu, this is Jenny. She's a new volunteer. Can you get a form for her to fill out and show her what we're doing with the envelopes?"

Lulu grunted and turned on her heel.

Jed rolled his eyes at Ashlynn. "Follow Lulu. She'll show you what to do."

Ashlynn nodded and joined Lulu at a table where

two other people were stuffing a folded sheet of paper into a preprinted envelope.

Lulu sat and shoved a chair toward Ashlynn with her foot. "Sit down. I don't know why Jed thinks someone needs to learn how to stuff envelopes, but if I sit here for a while with you, he'll stay off my back."

Ashlynn took the chair next to Lulu's. The longer she kept the surly campaign worker at the table, the longer she could avoid filling out any form.

Picking up a sheet of paper and an envelope, Ashlynn asked, "Don't you want to be here? I'm so excited about Councilwoman Escalante's chances. I think she'd be great for this city."

Lulu dug her elbows into the table and propped up her chin with her hands. "I'd rather be anywhere else, but my last name is Escalante. Veronica's my sister, so I sort of have to be here."

Ashlynn's pulse ticked up. Lulu could be a great source of information about the campaign and her sister. She shoved the paper into the envelope and raised her eyebrows. "Escalante? I thought the councilwoman was married."

"She's married to Kent Meadows. Can't get more Anglo than that." Lulu tapped her long, purple nails on the table. "But she keeps her maiden name to pretend she still cares about *la raza*. As if anyone from the old neighborhood is fooled. She's married to a freakin' billionaire."

Veronica's husband must be the same Meadows as Meadows Developments, who had signs and projects all over the city.

Lulu couldn't be a worse ambassador for her sister—and a better source of dirt. "What do you do when you're not helping your sister run for political office?"

"Mostly get into trouble." Lulu flipped her hair over her shoulder and laughed. "That's why she wants to keep me busy, but I don't think old Jed likes me here."

Ashlynn couldn't imagine why. "Oh, really?"

Lulu wasn't listening. Her gaze had traveled over Ashlynn's shoulder and her dark eyes sparkled. "*Hay, papi.* He's fine."

Ashlynn twisted her head to the side and froze as her gaze collided with Denver's stormy eyes.

Chapter Nine

Denver almost tripped over his own feet as he walked into Escalante's campaign headquarters and saw Ashlynn sitting there stuffing envelopes and chatting with a woman who looked like an escapee from the Kardashian compound.

But he didn't break his stride as he followed Jed Gordon to an office in the back of the room. What the hell was Ashlynn doing here? He hoped she'd planned on telling him about this little undercover stint—they had a deal.

"Please, have a seat, Detective. What can I do for you?" Gordon pointed to a chair across from a desk piled high with papers and folders.

Escalante's campaign headquarters buzzed but had nowhere near the activity of Mayor Wexler's office, and it didn't warrant his good suit. He fished his notebook from his pocket. "We have reason to believe Tiana Fuller, the victim of a homicide, worked for Councilwoman Escalante's campaign."

Gordon's black eyes flickered. Then he skimmed a hand over his shaved head. "That's terrible. Is this the same young woman who was found in the trunk of that car in the lake?"

"It is." Denver dropped his chin to his chest but didn't break eye contact with Gordon. "Did you know Tiana?"

"No." Gordon steepled his fingers and peered at Denver over the point. "We have a lot of volunteers, Detective. Some just wander in and out of this office, happy to do what they can to ensure a victory for Veronica."

Denver winced as he recognized one of Escalante's campaign slogans—Victory for Veronica. These political types never took a break.

"Maybe you'd recognize her face?" He slid the picture of Tiana her mother had provided from his pocket and positioned it on the desk, facing Gordon. "Does she look familiar?"

Gordon squinted at the picture as if bringing it into focus. "Pretty girl, but she doesn't look familiar to me. Like I said, we have a lot of volunteers coming off the streets to help out. Can I ask who gave you the information that this young woman worked for Veronica's campaign?"

"You can ask, but I can't tell you." Denver snatched the picture back. "Maybe some of the volunteers might recognize her."

Gordon blinked but not before his gaze shifted to the window on the busy room. "Sure. You can leave her picture here, and I'll ask around."

Denver pressed the picture to his chest. "I just

got this from her mother, and I have only one. I'll do the asking."

"Of course." Gordon pushed back his chair, all feigned eagerness.

"Before we go out there, can you provide me with a list of people who work for Councilwoman Escalante's campaign? Do you have a database of names or something?"

"We do." He brushed his fingers across his computer's keyboard. "I can have someone provide that for you."

"It must be a small list." Denver rested his hand on the doorknob and made a half turn.

"Small?" Gordon rubbed his hands together. "I assure you, we have a lot of volunteers on our team. We're much more grassroots than Mayor Wexler's campaign."

Denver wrinkled his brow, practicing his best dumb cop look. "Oh, you were so sure Tiana didn't work for Escalante's campaign, I thought you must know the names of all the volunteers."

Gordon's lips tightened for a second. "I'm sorry if I gave you the impression that Ms. Fuller never worked here. I just meant I'd never heard of her, nor seen her around the office."

"Okay. Maybe someone else has, or maybe her name will be on your list." Denver stepped out of the office and ignored Ashlynn.

He started on the other side of the room and flashed Tiana's picture to the volunteers, as Gordon stayed close, breathing down his neck.

He saved Ashlynn's station for last. He placed Tiana's photo in the middle of the table. "Have any of you ever seen this woman working here or at any events for Councilwoman Escalante?"

As they all shook their heads and murmured, a chair scraped against the floor. The woman Ashlynn had been talking to earlier, bumped against the table, shifting it.

She covered her mouth with her hand. "Oops, sorry."

Denver asked, "Have you seen her?"

"Me?" She flicked a long fingernail against what had to be fake eyelashes. "No."

Denver stepped back. "Okay. Thanks for your co-operation."

Gordon walked him to the door. "I'll email you that list of volunteers as soon as I get it, Detective Holt."

"Thank you for your cooperation." Denver shook the other man's hand.

As soon as he slid into his sedan, he texted Ashlynn to meet him for lunch someplace far far away from Escalante's campaign headquarters and the beady eyes of Jed Gordon. She had some explaining to do.

A half hour later, when he got to the almost-empty Mexican restaurant, he had the luxury of selecting a booth in the back. The waitress approached the table with a basket of chips and salsa. "Water?"

"Two, please, and I'll take a coffee."

By the time Ashlynn showed up, peering at him

through the dark restaurant, he'd munched through half the chips and downed his black coffee.

She paused at the table and studied the picture of Pancho Villa over their table. "Out of all the Mexican restaurants in LA, you picked this one?"

"Serves our purposes—big, dark, and nowhere near Escalante's headquarters." He pointed a chip at the seat across from him. "You wanna tell me what you were doing there?"

She plopped onto the vinyl banquette and gulped down some ice water. "Thought I'd do a little undercover investigation work."

"You're not afraid of getting recognized?"

"Did you see my picture anywhere on *LA Confidential*? It's not there for a reason. I don't do social media. Or, at least, I don't post any pictures of myself on my accounts." She grabbed a chip and dipped it in the salsa. "I'm not visible like a Megan Wright. Nobody there recognized Jenny Cochrane, or I'm sure Jed wouldn't have allowed me to stick around stuffing envelopes."

"He didn't ask you for ID or anything?"

"In case you didn't notice, that room wasn't exactly a beehive of activity, was it? Looks like they're a little short on volunteers." She waved her second chip in the air. "I was supposed to fill out some form with my name, address—that kind of thing—but I avoided it, and I'll keep on avoiding it."

"Keep on?" He stopped when the waitress hovered, asking if they were ready to order. He'd already studied the plastic menu and ordered a chicken burrito and a refill on his coffee.

Ashlynn ran her finger down the lunch specials. "I'll have the two chicken tacos, but can I get a side salad instead of rice and beans? And a diet whatever."

He leaned forward once the waitress left. "You plan to go back there?"

"I'm going to work the sister."

His hand holding the water glass jerked and the ice tinkled against the sides. "Sister?"

"Lourdes Escalante, goes by Lulu—black hair, long nails, eyelash extensions—total Kardashian vibe."

"That woman is Veronica Escalante's sister?"

"Sort of the black sheep, from what I can gather. No fan of her sister's." Ashlynn tilted her head and her ponytail swung over her shoulder. "Didn't you see what happened when you showed her the picture of Tiana?"

"The business with the chair?"

"That wasn't Lulu. That was Jed kicking the leg of her chair. I guess you couldn't see it because you were on the other side of the table. He was obviously warning her off talking about Tiana."

Denver wiped his hands on the napkin and dropped it back in his lap. "It didn't seem like the others knew Tiana because Jed didn't have to warn any of them."

"I don't know." She shrugged. "Lulu's going to be closer to the inner workings of the campaign, whether she likes it or not—and she doesn't. She hates working there."

Denver chewed on his bottom lip. "They might be hiding the fact that Tiana worked there to distance themselves from her murder, but wouldn't Tiana have told someone about working for the campaign? I'm meeting with her parents this afternoon. I'll ask them about it."

The waitress returned with their food, sliding his burrito in front of him and refilling his coffee.

As Ashlynn fluffed up her salad with her fork, she wrinkled her nose. "That's a huge burrito, and it's almost too early for lunch."

"Tell me about it, but I figured it would be less crowded here at eleven, and I wanted to talk to you before I met with Mr. and Mrs. Edmonds." He sliced the end off his burrito and steam rose, warning him to back off. "I'm glad I did. I didn't even notice Jed nudging Lulu's chair. She complied, though, didn't she? Kept mum about Tiana."

"Not for long." She poked her chest with the end of her fork. "I'm going to get it out of her."

"How do you plan to do that? Especially if Jed is hovering in the background."

"He's busy in the office, on the phone. He doesn't have time to watch Lulu, and he has no reason to suspect I'm after anything but the thrill of working on a political campaign."

He smirked at her fresh face. "Laid it on thick, huh?"

"I did, and I know just how to get Lulu to open up. I pretended to be slightly shocked by every little thing she said today, and she enjoyed the effect her words had on me. I'll keep that up. Keep supplying the drama for her and she'll keep opening up more and more. Lulu doesn't much like her brother-in-law, either, Kent Meadows. *The* Kent Meadows."

Denver whistled. "His name is plastered all over the city. You'd think Veronica would want to use it for name recognition alone."

"Not sure about that, but according to Lulu, Kent is backing his wife's political aspirations."

"You *did* get a lot out of Lulu. Maybe you missed your calling. Instead of a journalist, you should've been a therapist."

The corner of her eye twitched. "No, thanks. I've had enough of those."

He avoided her gaze and sawed off another piece of his burrito. She seemed too well adjusted to require the services of a therapist. But what did he know? The department had been telling him for years to see a shrink, and he thought he was pretty balanced, too. At least once he stopped caring about anyone enough to obsessively worry, he'd been fine.

"Nothing more on your blog? Anyone talking about Lil' Snoop's claim that Tiana worked for the Escalante campaign?"

"Just more political intrigue theories. Wait until they find out about the CREW car. Are you releasing that information?"

"We are. It's going to get out anyway. The parking attendant in the building where the CREW is located already knows something is up. And once the mainstream media—no offense—pick up the story about Tiana possibly working for Escalante, things are going to heat up in the mayor's race."

She held up her taco, which dripped onto her plate. "No offense taken. If the LAPD can't verify that Tiana worked there, though, they may drop the story. If Jed doesn't have a record of Tiana being a volunteer or her parents don't confirm she worked there, it may be a nonstory."

"Or people will confuse the campaigns when they find out the car was from Wexler's. They might think she volunteered for Wexler."

She crunched into her taco and a shower of shredded lettuce fell to her plate. "It is a coincidence, though, isn't it? I mean, maybe her death has nothing to do with the campaigns."

"Maybe." He lifted his shoulders. "But even if another campaign worker murdered her for personal reasons, it ain't gonna look good for the candidate."

"Politics is a dirty business." She dabbed her mouth with a napkin, leaving a string of lettuce in the wisps of hair framing her face.

He reached forward and plucked it free. Holding it up on his finger, he said, "Lettuce in your hair."

"Yikes, can't take me anywhere."

He'd take her anywhere and everywhere. Maybe he needed to take a step back and evaluate why he'd agreed to cooperate with her. Was it because of Tiana and the case, or because he just wanted to be close to her?

He didn't need to be close to her—or anyone.

"Almost done?" He pushed away his plate with the half-eaten burrito.

She had just crunched into her second taco and waved her hand in front of her mouth as she chewed. She swallowed and took a sip of her soda. "You're done already? I'd like to finish this taco."

"You were right. It is too early to eat lunch. I'll take this with me and finish it at my desk." He checked his phone. "I gotta go back to the station right now and write up a few things before meeting with Tiana's mom and stepdad."

Ashlynn's face blanched and her lush lips tightened into a frown. "You go ahead. I'm going to finish my lunch."

As he tossed his napkin on the table and reached for his wallet, she held out her hand. "That's okay. I'll take care of the bill."

He plucked out a twenty and a ten and dropped them on the table. "I got it. You paid for dinner last night, and you gave me some good info today."

She dragged her napkin from her lap and pressed it against her chest. "You don't have to pay me for information."

"I didn't mean it like that. I'll touch base later, if I have anything else to share." He stood and raised his hand. "Take care, Ashlynn."

He spun around and walked blindly toward the exit as Ashlynn called after him. "You forgot your burrito."

He'd forgotten more than his burrito. He'd forgotten his vow never to care for anyone ever again—at least, nobody alive.

Chapter Ten

Ashlynn's nose stung as she dabbed the tip of her finger on a drop of hot sauce in her plate. "Jerk."

The guy had done a one-eighty on her—one minute scarfing down chips and salsa and discussing the case with her, the next throwing down his napkin and practically running for the exit.

She sighed and poked her fork at her unfinished taco. He'd probably prefer to work with Sean, too. She'd had no business taking over *LA Confidential*. She would never reach the heights Sean had reached.

She dropped the fork and squared her shoulders. *Stop doing this to yourself, Ashlynn...and eat.* Detective Holt wasn't anything special—arrogant, hostile— and she could see through it all to the part of him that desperately wanted to be a full-fledged homicide detective.

She scooped up her taco and took a big bite with a smile on her face. She'd uncovered a lot more about this case than he had. What had he given her? The pleasure of his company, that's it. And that hadn't turned out to be much.

Shoving the rest of the taco in her mouth, she waved to the waitress. "Can you please bring me a box for this burrito?"

"Sure." She pointed at the money on the table. "Do you want me to take this?"

"Yes." Ashlynn leaned back against the banquette and patted her full stomach. He'd just paid for her lunch *and* her dinner.

BY THE TIME she'd made it home after running a few errands, proofreading her freelance article on public art spaces in LA, and having an online meeting with her web designer, Denver's burrito had turned into a soggy mess. She'd dumped the whole thing in her sink and run the disposal with gusto.

He hadn't contacted her the rest of the day, so she didn't know how his meeting with Tiana's parents had lasted—not that he owed her anything. In fact, it seemed as if he didn't think he owed her anything at all.

This relationship had been a one-way street—in many ways.

She swung open the fridge door and surveyed the packed shelves. After she'd recovered from her eating disorder, her therapist had recommended that she keep food in her kitchen—healthy stuff. She just figured she'd have some of that stir-fry left, so she wouldn't have to cook again tonight. But Denver Holt had gobbled up everything in sight last night—everything but her. She slammed the fridge door shut.

One night of In-N-Out with animal fries wasn't

going to make her relapse. As she grabbed her keys, her cell phone buzzed.

Her heart flip-flopped in her chest when she saw Lulu's name. The two of them had exchanged numbers while working together today. She'd given Lulu her real number, as she didn't mention *LA Confidential* on her voice-mail greeting for this phone. She kept a separate phone for the blog.

She pitched her voice higher with an excitement she didn't have to fake. "Hi, Lulu. Wassup?"

"Girl, you left the building so fast, I didn't get a chance to tell you about the fundraiser tonight."

"Fundraiser?" Her voice positively squeaked.

"It's the best part of working for this stupid campaign—the only good part. All the volunteers are always invited to the fundraisers. I'm not saying we don't have to run around like gofers sometimes, but the food's usually good, there's valet parking, and the booze is first rate…and free. Can't get better than that."

"Perfect. I'm always down for free booze. Where and when? And are you sure it's okay if I'm there? I just started today. For all you know, I might never come back."

"I don't care about that, and Jed's not gonna notice you one way or the other—not with my sister in the room." Lulu huffed out a breath. "The fundraiser is at my sister's house in Sherman Oaks. It's up in the hills, off Beverly Glen with all the other mansions. I'll text you the address. It starts at seven, but show up closer to eight when it'll be more crowded."

"So I can sneak in? Are you sure it's okay?" she asked again, unsure.

"You're not sneaking. You're a volunteer. Grass-roots and all that. It's just that the food will be circulating by then, and it's easier to snag drinks without certain people watching you."

All of a sudden, Ashlynn was starving. "Sounds dank. What should I wear?"

"If you're looking for a sugar daddy, you can go slinky cocktail. If you wanna come off as the dedicated kiss-ass, dress down from there."

"Thanks for thinking of me, Lulu. I can squeeze in a little more studying by eight. You'll be there by then?"

"I'm already here. I live in this hellhole known as my sister's house."

As soon as they ended the call, Lulu texted her Veronica's address. Lulu had just presented her with the perfect opportunity to get close to the Escalante campaign. Nobody there would know her face.

She scanned through her contacts for Denver's personal cell. Her finger hovered over his name for a second, and then she tossed the phone onto the kitchen counter. If he wanted to cool things down, she could be ice cold.

In the end, she dressed somewhere between sugar baby and earnest young volunteer. She straightened the hem of her little black dress and stepped into the black sandals, waiting in front of the mirror. She released her hair from her ponytail and fluffed it around her shoulders.

When she slid behind the wheel of her car, she tapped in the address for Veronica Escalante's house. If the GPS took her by way of the Valley, she'd force it to change. Even at this time of night, she didn't want to chance traffic out to the Valley. She'd go up the back way and take Mulholland.

Forty-five minutes later, Ashlynn negotiated the hairpin turns on Mulholland to reach Escalante's house in the hills. She rolled to a stop behind a line of cars waiting for the valet parking attendants.

How much money would Escalante raise to ultimately lose to Mayor Wexler? What would her campaign do to make sure she didn't lose?

An attendant in a white shirt and red vest jogged up to her car and she popped the locks. He opened her door. "Good evening, miss."

That was a nice touch. "Hello. Just leave the keys in the ignition?"

"Yes, miss. We'll take care of your car."

She surveyed the gleaming luxury vehicles ahead and behind her in the line. She had a lot less to worry about with her VW than the rest of these well-heeled donors. "I'm sure you will. Thanks."

As she exited the car, she hitched her small black purse across her body. Her heels crunched the gravel as she made her way toward the gates of the house until she hit the pavers on the circular driveway.

The double doors stood open and lights bathed the beautiful garden in front. Ashlynn inhaled the heady scent of jasmine and ducked behind a couple approaching the broad steps fronting the Tudor-style mansion.

Who knew sitting on the LA city council paid so well? But then, Veronica had her own, private wealthy donor.

As soon as she and the couple made it over the threshold, a waiter appeared, bearing a tray of champagne flutes glimmering with the golden liquid. Ashlynn lifted a glass and took a small sip while sidling against a wall to take in the spectacle.

She'd never moved in political circles and neither had her parents, despite their wealth, but these folks knew how to live it up. She snatched a little pastry puff of something from a tray that floated by and stuffed it into her mouth. Shrimp. She hadn't eaten since she'd forced herself to finish that taco from her early lunch with Denver.

She zigzagged her way through the crowd to reach the pretty display of food and lifted a small plate from the stack.

"Told you." Lulu appeared next to her, dressed to kill in a slinky red number with cutouts along the sides and a deep V, clinging to all of Lulu's dangerous curves. "The food is worth the boredom."

"You don't look like you're planning on boredom." Ashlynn piled a few shrimp puffs on her plate, some bacon-wrapped scallops, a couple of tiny ribs and a piece of bruschetta.

Lulu winked. "Sometimes you get lucky."

"Does your sister know you troll for—" Ashlynn waved the bread in the air "—luck at her fundraisers?"

"How do you think she snagged her rich husband? He's gotta have at least twenty years on her. So, as long as I keep it hush-hush, she doesn't care what I do." Lulu narrowed her heavily made-up eyes. "She hates publicity—the bad kind."

Like a campaign volunteer showing up dead in the trunk of a submerged car.

"Who doesn't?" Ashlynn licked some barbecue sauce from her finger and grabbed a napkin. "You don't have to babysit me. I'm gonna make my way through this food, grab a few more glasses of champagne, and flirt with that bartender."

"Don't sell yourself short. You're cute in a wholesome kind of way. These older guys vibe on that." Lulu smoothed her dress over her hips and shimmied her shoulders. "I got a line on one now."

Ashlynn watched Lulu sashay across the room toward a huddle of men old enough to be her father. At least Lulu's game plan would leave her alone long enough to snoop around.

As she stood with her plate, shoveling enough little appetizers in her mouth to make up a three-course meal, Ashlynn sized up the room. She could distinguish the donors from the hangers-on or charity cases by their clothing, and Veronica Escalante was no slouch as a clotheshorse. Ashlynn could spot the councilwoman's designer shoes with the red soles, as she worked her way through the crowd schmoozing.

Ashlynn hadn't been lying to Denver when she'd told him she'd written fashion articles for an e-magazine, but she hadn't told him she knew clothes inside and out because her mother had been a model. Her mother had lived and breathed fashion, and had tried to make it the center of Ashlynn's life, too.

She'd fallen short, literally by one inch, of her mom's willowy five-foot-ten-inch frame, which had only increased her mother's pressure on her to stay thin.

She'd showed her. Ashlynn had become a pro at staying thin.

Ashlynn had left her champagne glass at the end of the table where she'd started, but had no desire to finish the drink. She stashed her empty plate on a tray by the door and asked the cute bartender for a Coke with a lime on the side.

She'd already spotted the other volunteers and made her way to where they stood in a clump by the patio door, which led to a sparkling pool. She hung on the edge of the group, her hand curled around the highball glass.

A lull in their conversation offered her an in. She cleared her throat. "What did you all think about that cop flashing that girl's picture around this afternoon?"

One of the guys glanced her way, and a spark of recognition lit his dark eyes. "Oh, you just started today, huh?"

"Yeah, that's me." She raised her hand as if she were sitting in a classroom. "The new girl."

The man patted his chest. "I'm Andre. This is Sydney, Bryant, and Karis."

"I'm Jenny." Ashlynn nodded to the group, raising her glass.

Sydney, a young woman with a sleek, blond ponytail, definitely dressed for eager political asset, asked. "You work fast. Your first day and you made it to a gala."

"Lulu invited me today."

Sydney's eyes widened. "Lulu invited you here?"

"Y-yeah. Should I not be here?"

"No, we're always invited. It's just that Lulu isn't the friendliest person in the office." Sydney cupped a hand around her mouth. "You know she's Veronica's sister, right?"

"I do. She was friendly to me." Ashlynn plucked the lime from the edge of her glass and squeezed it into the Coke. "I guess nobody knew the girl in that picture."

Andre patted the side of his short Afro. "We didn't know her, but we knew who she was—that murdered girl. We still can't figure out why the po-po came around asking questions."

Ashlynn tipped her head and wrinkled her nose. "I think I heard the cop say something to Jed about that girl working for Veronica's campaign."

Karis, the petite Latina, grabbed Sydney's arm "No way. She worked for Veronica? I never saw her in the office."

"That's crap." Bryant finally spoke, pushing his hipster black-rimmed glasses up on his nose. "None of us ever saw her. She didn't work for the campaign. Maybe she was one of those wannabes who get all excited and then lose interest after they make one phone call. They come and go. How about you, Jenny? You a wannabe?"

"Me?" Ashlynn put her hand over her heart. "I'm all-in."

She jiggled the ice in her drink and took a sip. No Jed here to coach them. They honestly didn't know Tiana, had never seen her at the office, but that didn't mean Lulu didn't know the dead woman. She hadn't imagined Jed's nudge to the chair when Denver showed Lulu Tiana's picture.

"If you are sticking around, here's a pro tip." Karis tapped her finger against her head. "Stay away from Kent."

Ashlynn widened her eyes as her pulse jumped. "Kent Meadows, Veronica's husband."

"Yeah, he's a creeper." Karis hugged herself. "Right, Sydney?"

The blonde nodded solemnly. "Total manther."

"'Manther'?" Ashlynn had to show her ignorance if she wanted the answer.

Karis giggled and tossed her dark curls. "You know. Instead of a cougar, an older woman going after young guys, he's a manther. Cougar...panther... manther."

Ashlynn wrinkled her nose. "Yuck."

Sydney waved her drink toward the patio. "I see someone lighting up on the other side of the pool. Anyone want to keep me company?"

Bryant answered, "Only if you let me bum a ciggie off you."

As the two of them wandered off, Ashlynn jerked her thumb over her shoulder. "I'm going to get some more free booze before they cut us off."

If Lulu was the one who knew about Tiana, then she should be talking to Lulu. She propped up the wall next to the bar and scanned the room, her gaze meeting Jed's for a split second.

His ankle-length slacks and no-socks ensemble screamed, *I'm trying hard to look fresh.* But at least he glanced away, not recognizing her, and she turned her head so he wouldn't catch her on the double-take—not that she didn't have every right to be there. The other volunteers had showed up, and she'd been personally invited by Lulu, although there didn't seem to be any love lost between Lulu and Jed.

She spied Lulu chatting up an older man in a pair of nice slacks, a black T and a mustard-colored jacket. It worked. He looked put together with a personal twist. He stroked his salt-and-pepper beard, while leaning toward Lulu and her cleavage.

Ashlynn gripped her glass and threaded her way through the crowd to reach Lulu and her conquest.

Attaching herself to the duo, she said, "Great turnout."

Lulu's seductive stance changed in a second as she gave Ashlynn a pointed look. "Yeah, great. Jenny, this is Syngin Parish. Syngin, one of our volunteers."

"Nice to meet you, Jenny." Syngin gave her hand the briefest of squeezes before dropping it. He wanted her gone as much as Lulu did.

"You, too. Thanks for supporting Councilwoman Escalante. She'll do great things for the city."

Syngin's blue eyes sparkled with amusement. "I've known Veronica's husband, Kent Meadows, for years. I'm afraid I'm not very political."

"Everyone needs the support of friends." She winked.

Lulu drilled a knuckle into Ashlynn's back. "You should go find Jed and show him your face for a few brownie points."

"Oh, I will." She put a finger on her chin. "Speaking of the office, did Lulu tell you that a LAPD detective came to the campaign headquarters today asking if we knew that murdered girl, Tiana Fuller?"

Syngin's face didn't register any change at all, but Lulu stiffened beside her.

"I didn't hear that. I heard about the body in the lake, but I didn't know she was connected to the campaign."

"Because she's not." Lulu squeezed Ashlynn's upper arm, her long nails digging into her flesh. "If you actually want to help the campaign, Jenny, you won't talk about murders."

Ashlynn covered her mouth with her hand. "I'm so sorry. I just thought it was weird he was there. Nobody knew her, so he must've been wrong."

Syngin flashed his very white teeth. "You don't have to worry about me. As I said, I'm apolitical. I'm just here to support Kent and Veronica—and because I have lots of money."

"I knew there was something I liked about you."

Lulu tugged on the sleeve of the mustard jacket, fluttering her lash extensions.

Ashlynn had never felt more like a third wheel. "I'm going to find Jed, grab some more food and head out. Thanks for the invite, Lulu."

Syngin and Lulu barely noticed her departure as she slipped back into the crowd. She didn't want to draw Jed's attention to her, but it sounded like Lulu would tell him she was at the party, anyway. She might as well touch base.

She studied each knot of people and those wandering in and out of the house. Was Jed a smoker? She stepped outside onto the patio and stood at the water's edge, squinting at the smokers across the pool.

A leaf drifted from one of the trees, which must create a natural umbrella for the patio, and landed in the water. Ashlynn meandered around the curve of the pool and ducked down, scooping the leaf from the lapping water with her hand.

Before she rose from her crouch, she heard whispers from the clump of trees. Holding her breath, she stayed down and strained to hear the voices. A man and a woman went back and forth in heated conversation, but she couldn't make out the words.

Twisting her head, she peered to the side, just getting a glimpse of two pairs of legs. She made out a man in high-cut black slacks, no socks and brown loafers, and a woman in a dress or skirt, long bare legs, her feet in a pair of expensive stilettos. Ashlynn could see the red soles in the dark.

She crawled a few feet away from the trees and rose to a standing position, brushing off her knees. She didn't want to get caught eavesdropping on Jed and Veronica.

Why were they arguing in secret? Better than arguing in public, but why would those two be arguing? Jed was her campaign manager. Veronica's word should be law.

She heard the bushes rustle behind her but she didn't turn around. Instead, she adjusted her purse across her body and dug inside for her valet ticket and a five-dollar bill.

She cruised through the house, giving a quick wave to Lulu and then landing on the front porch. Clutching her ticket and cash, she approached the valet attendants.

"Hey, can I get my car, please?"

One of the young men sprang forward with his hand held out, and she placed the ticket in his palm. His shoes crunched against the road as he scurried off to find her car.

This neighborhood in the hills south of Ventura Boulevard didn't need sidewalks. These streets were for residents only, not scraggly pedestrians who didn't have any business in this hood. Apparently, they didn't need streetlamps, either.

Ashlynn rubbed her arms as she waited for her car, Ranchera music thumping from a speaker where the valets huddled.

She stepped forward as the attendant pulled her

car up in front of her. He left the engine running and the door open.

"Thanks." She slipped him the five and got behind the wheel. Hopefully, the parking attendants would be getting better tips from the likes of Syngin, but she knew rich people. They could be cheaper than anyone. She hoped, for Lulu's sake, Syngin wasn't one of those stingy ones.

She pulled onto the road and turned toward Mulholland Drive again. Even with the twists and turns on this part of the road, she preferred it to going through the Valley. And she'd had only two sips of champagne and a boatload of food. She'd be fine.

She negotiated the first few turns with ease before noticing the headlights behind her. Damn. She was more comfortable driving these kinds of roads if nobody was behind her. She tapped her rearview mirror and said, "You're gonna have to relax, buddy. I'm not whizzing around these curves."

She eased off the accelerator at the next bend but instead of backing off, the car behind her got right on her tail. There were no immediate turnouts for her to allow him to pass. She muttered, "Moron."

She came out of the turn and sped up a little, but the next curve greeted her all too soon. She slowed again, and the guy behind her was not having it.

His headlights flooded her car as he rode her bumper.

"What is your problem?" She hugged the shoulder on the right in case he wanted to risk passing her. Sure enough, he moved into the opposing lane of traffic, but instead of roaring ahead like she'd expected, his car bumped the back of hers.

She grabbed the wheel but her tires were already on gravel and they spun to gain purchase on the shifting surface.

The last thing she saw before rolling down the canyon was the other car's taillights as it sped away.

Chapter Eleven

Denver slid down further in his seat and shielded his eyes against the oncoming headlights of Ashlynn's car. Either she'd found what she'd needed or realized she wasn't going to get anything out of Escalante's donors—and she hadn't even told him about her plans.

He didn't deserve to know after the way he'd treated her at lunch. His scheme had worked the way he'd intended: give her the cold shoulder, make her dismiss him as a jerk and throw cold water on whatever they had going on.

Another vehicle crawled out from a shallow turnout, its parking lights barely illuminating the road. Had the valet attendants been using that space for the guests' cars?

His senses percolated as he watched the low-key car roll past the valet stand and Escalante's house. Why was the driver creeping around? Taking license numbers?

He flicked his rearview and watched the car make the same turn toward Mulholland as Ashlynn had made. He swallowed against his dry throat. Was someone tailing her?

He cranked on his engine and made a tight U-turn in the road, waving out the window at the valets who'd let him park across the street after he'd flashed his badge and given each of them a twenty. He made the turn onto Mulholland just in time to see the taillights of the sedan, which had taken off after Ashlynn's, disappear around the first bend of a winding section of the boulevard.

He sped up, but the car was keeping well ahead of his. Crazy driving.

Coming out of the next curve, Denver blinked his eyes. The reverse lights of the black sedan he'd been following glowed as the driver backed up on the road. Beyond the trunk, Ashlynn's car poked over the edge of the canyon at a forty-five-degree angle.

The stealth car switched into Drive and started rolling toward Ashlynn's precariously situated vehicle. Denver flashed his headlights and flicked on his blue and red revolvers.

The driver of the sedan jerked to the right and, with a squeal of tires, shot off down the road.

Denver had gotten a partial plate, but he couldn't leave Ashlynn's vehicle at the precipice of the canyon. He hadn't seen any movement from the VW, and his heart pounded as he parked his own vehicle, killing the lights, and clambered out of it.

He rushed to the edge of the road where Ashlynn's car pointed toward the canyon, his shoes slipping on the gravel, almost carrying him past the car and into the trees.

Grabbing on to her door handle, he peered inside the window. Her head turned toward him, her eyes wide and glassy, her hands still gripping her steering wheel.

All four of her wheels were still on solid ground—just—and he yanked open her door. "Are you hurt?"

"I—I don't think so."

"Turn off your engine. Put the car in Park. Can you do that?" He reached across her body and unhitched her seat belt.

She shoved the gearshift into Park and switched off the ignition. Then she placed her hands back on the wheel.

He touched her wrist gently. "You can get out of the car, Ashlynn. It's okay. It's not gonna go over or shift if you move."

She released the steering wheel as if it burned her hands and whipped her head around to face him, her hair dancing at her shoulders like flames. "A car forced me off the road and took off."

"I figured that. I saw the tail end of the accident." He didn't tell her he thought the car was getting ready to push her into the canyon. "The sedan took off."

"Bastard." Her anger broke through her shock and she scrambled out of her car, landing on her knees.

"Steady." He took her arm and helped her to her feet. He glanced at her high-heeled, strappy sandals and swept her into his arms to carry her up to the road.

"I can walk." She kicked her legs.

He set her down on the side of the road. "I know that, but that's some rocky ground. I slipped myself, and I'm not wearing sexy sandals."

Her chin dropped and she stared at her black dress, as if she'd forgotten what she was wearing.

"Are you all right?" He fished into his pocket for his phone. "I'm calling 9-1-1."

"Don't!" She grabbed his arm. "If you make a fuss here, the people from the party might find out about this. I attended that fundraiser as Jenny, ingenue college student and starry-eyed political volunteer. I'd have to give the police my real name."

"You can't leave your car there. You can't back it out of there without risking it tumbling down the canyon—with you in it."

She covered her mouth. "That's what he wanted. He pushed me off the road. He just didn't push hard enough."

"What happened in there?" He jerked his thumb back toward Escalante's house.

"Wait." She ran a pair of unsteady hands through her hair. "What are you doing here? Did you follow me again?"

"I didn't follow you. I didn't even know you were going to be here." He waved at a car slowing toward them to go ahead. Ashlynn was right. They didn't need a collection of cars and people up here. "I knew about the fundraiser and thought I'd do a little surveillance to see who showed up. I saw you arrive, and figured you were here as your alter ego. Then when I saw you leave, I noticed a suspicious car hot on your tail. I'm glad my instincts kicked in."

"Me, too." She folded her arms and kicked some pebbles with her toe.

She still thought he was a jerk, and that was okay.

"But we need to make sure you're okay…and get your car out of here."

"Don't I look okay?" She spread her arms wide, and his gaze swept over her body in her short black dress, long, slim legs up to there.

He dragged his eyes to her face. "You look fine. Why didn't your airbags deploy?"

"No clue. Maybe because I didn't hit anything? It was like a roll down the hill." She rubbed the back of her neck. "Just noticing a little soreness back here, maybe whiplash."

"Probably. You need to a see a doctor."

"I'll see my own doctor, in my own time. Are you gonna help me get my car out of here?"

"What? Push it up the hill with my bare hands?"

"You know…people, don't you? Can't we do this on the hush-hush? If the cops come out here with their lights and sirens and tow trucks and ambulances, it's going to cause a scene. People leaving the party are bound to stop. I'll have to tell the cops where I was. They might even give me a breathalyzer."

He cut her off. "Have you been drinking?"

"Do two sips of champagne count? No, I haven't been drinking, but the cops might want to check out

the party. I can't afford that, Denver. I can't afford
to blow my cover."

"You already did." He clenched his teeth. He'd
like to get his hands on the person driving that sedan.

Ashlynn caught her bottom lip between her teeth.
"You're right about that. Either someone followed me
to Escalante's, or someone made me there."

Another two cars wound down the road, and Denver waved them past. "We need to get out of here
before more people leave the party. My guess is the
majority won't take Mulholland, but enough will."

"So, you agree we shouldn't create a scene here."

"Do you promise me you'll see a doctor about
your neck?"

"Promise." She drew a cross over her heart.

"Okay, hop in my car, and I'll get you home, as
long as you tell me what you discovered at the fundraiser." He took her arm to guide her to his vehicle
tucked into a small outlet.

She slipped from his grasp when she reached the
car. "So, now there are two conditions? I go to the
doctor and give up what I discovered? When do I
get something out of this relationship besides a ride
home?"

Opening the passenger door, he held up two fingers. "If we're keeping track here, I've rescued you
twice now—three times if we're counting the break-
in at your house and the message on your mirror."

"That wasn't a rescue. That was moral support."
She dropped onto the seat and slammed the door.

He blew out a breath and circled to the driver's

side. When he got in behind the wheel, he slid a gaze to the side. Ashlynn had her eyes closed.

"You're sure you're okay?"

"I probably could use some ibuprofen." She massaged her temples.

"You're in luck." He flipped up the console and felt around for the small bottle every detective kept in every car. His fingers closed around it and he shook it before handing the bottle to Ashlynn. "You can take it down with my lukewarm coffee, if you like."

"Thanks." She popped the lid, shook a green gel cap into her palm and slapped her hand against her mouth. She plucked his cup from the holder and took a small sip, leaving a semicircle of red lipstick on the lid.

He maneuvered his car back onto the road. "I'll call the tow service we use tonight. I don't think anyone's going to see your car off the road in the meantime. I only knew it was there because I saw you roll over the edge and your lights were still on."

"I hope nobody calls it in." She settled into the seat and tucked her hands between her knees. "You wanna know what I discovered at the party?"

"If you're ready." His muscles tensed. Had she been asking too many questions at the fundraiser?

She held up her hand and ticked off each item on her fingers. "I don't think any of the volunteers know about Tiana Fuller. I think Lulu does know something about Tiana, and so does Jed. Jed and Veronica seem to have something more going on than candidate and campaign manager."

"How'd you determine that last bit?"

"I heard them in a heated discussion out by the pool, under cover."

A muscle twitched in his jaw. "Did you hear what they said?"

"Nope. Whispers, and I didn't want to get too close."

He released a breath. "They didn't see you?"

"Not sure about that."

"That's all you got?"

"That and the definition of manther."

He snorted. "Enlighten me."

"A manther is like a male cougar—an older man who hits on younger women. The volunteers said Kent Meadows was a manther." She slugged his arm. "Don't ever become a manther."

"Don't worry about that. I prefer women to girls." He cleared his throat. "Anything else?"

She pulled her skirt over her thighs. "That and a closer relationship with Lulu. She's the one who invited me to the party. She called me."

"Do you think you can get more out of her?"

"Maybe." She gathered her hair in one hand, dragging it over her shoulder. "But I'd kind of like to get more out of you."

His head jerked to the side. "What do you mean?"

"Don't get excited." She patted his forearm. "I don't mean more warmth or humanity. I'm talking about your meeting with Tiana's parents. You met with them after lunch and didn't bother to fill me in at all. This is beginning to feel like a one-way street."

Should he tell her he'd changed his mind about

their deal? Or at least he had until he'd seen her glide up Escalante's driveway like she owned the place. He couldn't deny having a source like Ashlynn might help him solve Tiana's murder.

He cleared his throat. "I'll tell you about it when we get back to your place."

Closing her eyes, she nodded. "Deal."

And just like that, Ashlynn Hughes was back in his life.

BY THE TIME Ashlynn pushed open the door to her place, she could barely move her head on her stiff neck. She'd taken an ibuprofen in the car, but she needed another.

"Do you want something to drink? I'm going to pop another pill and put some ice on my neck." She hung on to the freezer door. "Ice or heat?"

"I'd start with ice, but I'm no expert." He sidled up next to her at the fridge and said, "Bottled water or tap?"

"I use the water from the refrigerator. I figure it's filtered, and I haven't grown any horns yet."

He brushed past her and lifted two glasses from her cupboard. "Ice to go with your ice?"

"No, thanks." She crouched next to the fridge and pulled a plastic bag from a drawer. "I'm going to fill this with ice and deposit it against the back of my neck. I guess it could've been worse, huh?"

"Are you going to tell me what happened at that fundraiser to make someone come after you and try to run you off the road?"

"I told you everything that happened. I did not draw attention to myself." She punched the button on the ice maker to release the ice and fill her bag.

"Someone noticed you, or someone recognized you. You run one of the most popular blogs in the city. Why do you think you can run around incognito?" He took her place in front of the fridge and filled up two glasses with water.

"*LA Confidential* is not really my blog. I didn't make it popular. That was Sean's doing."

He cocked his head at her. "Take credit where credit is due. Your brother is gone, and you've done a helluva job in his place. That series you did on Reed Dufrain and the shenanigans at the Brighter Day Recovery Center was top-notch. That drug lab sounded like something from a TV show. You did that, Ashlynn. Why are you selling yourself short?"

She shrugged and her bag of ice crackled against her neck. "Just feels like it's Sean's baby, like it'll never be mine."

"Make it your own, or do something else. I thought you said something about a podcast?"

"Yeah, Sean intended to turn *LA Confidential* into a podcast. I had started helping him."

"Take the idea and run with it." He placed his hand on the small of her back and steered her toward the couch. "Sit down, and I'll tell you what I found out from Tiana's parents."

She lowered herself to the cushion on the end, positioning the bag on her neck. "Was it hard talking to them?"

"Hard for me?" His eyebrows shot up to his hairline and the dark lock of hair that had a habit of falling across his forehead. "What I feel is nothing compared to what they're going through."

She nodded. "I remember when the detective came to tell me about my brother's murder. He was so uncomfortable, I almost felt like I was supposed to comfort him. I didn't want to break down too much because I was afraid of what it would do to him."

"It shouldn't be that way. As difficult as it is for us, it's not our tragedy, not our story." He coughed and gulped back some water. "Tiana's parents couldn't tell me much, but I got the impression that she *was* working for the Escalante campaign."

"Just an impression?" The ice slipped to her shoulder and she left it. "They couldn't tell you for sure?"

"They didn't know for sure, but Tiana was a political science major at Cal State Long Beach. She was very interested in local politics, and was looking forward to applying for an internship with the city of Long Beach her senior year. It would make sense that she'd volunteer for a campaign like Escalante's."

"But she never specifically told her parents she was working for Escalante?"

"Nope." Denver scratched his jaw. "I wonder why. If she were so excited about politics, you'd think she'd tell her parents about her volunteer work."

"She was keeping it a secret for some reason." She snapped her fingers. "What about Wexler's campaign? Did they ever get back to you with a list of their volunteers?"

"They did, but her name wasn't on the list. I wasn't anticipating it. If she'd been working for them, I would expect them to scrub her name from the database. Tiana is already connected to one of their cars, they don't want to compound the problem by linking her to the campaign."

Ashley wrinkled her nose. "Tiana is working for Escalante and winds up dead in a vehicle tied to the Wexler campaign."

"Doesn't make any sense." Denver massaged his temples. "Oh, and her mother said Tiana had a boyfriend up here, or maybe just a guy who was a friend—Tony Fuentes."

"He hasn't contacted you?"

"No, but I'm going to run him down and find out why." He pointed to her plastic bag. "That's slipping down your arm. I thought you had whiplash."

"It's too cold." She snatched the bag from her shoulder, cupping it in her palms.

"That's kind of the point." He took the ice from her hands and said, "Turn around."

She presented her back to him, tucking one leg beneath her and tugging her dress over her thighs.

Denver swept her hair over her shoulder, his fingers trailing along her bare back.

A warm flush suffused her body. If he put that ice against her skin now, it would melt in a matter of seconds.

The ice clacked as he positioned it on the back of her neck. He kept his hand on the bag, pressing it against all the stiff spots. She closed her eyes as a chilling numbness seemed to freeze her twitching muscles.

"Okay, yeah. I see the point here." She lifted her shoulders and shivered. "It hurts so good. I mean I kind of can't stand it, but the ice is definitely numbing the area."

"I think we were right to ice instead of heat." He blew out a warm breath that tickled her flesh. "I was relieved to see you weren't hurt—at least not seriously. When I saw that car take off after yours, I didn't think he was going to run you off the road. Follow you, maybe, but he could've killed you."

Ashlynn jerked her head to the side and clamped her neck with a wince. "Do you think whoever is threatening me graduated to violence?"

He dropped the bag of ice to the coffee table. "I think he already did that in Venice."

"I'm talking about mortal violence. You think someone wants to kill me?"

His hand skimmed down her back. "He pushed you into a shallow dip, not off the edge of a canyon. He could've picked a more dangerous spot on Mulholland to start playing bumper cars with you. I think you're still in the warning stage. It's not like you've discovered anything about Tiana yet. Neither have we."

He'd been rubbing a circle on her back, and her eyelashes fluttered when he stopped. "Could you keep doing that?"

She felt his warmth behind her as he gathered her hair in her hand and lifted it from her neck. He pressed his lips against her cool flesh and she could almost feel the sizzle.

"Yeah, like that." She dipped her head and his lips trailed to her collarbone.

Turning to face him, she grabbed the lapels of his denim jacket. "You always seem to be in the right place at the right time to rescue me."

"Right place, but always two beats late." His lips crooked into a smile and the unexpectedness of it took her breath away.

She smoothed her hands against the front of his T-shirt, and his heart thumped beneath her palms, matching the pulse in her fingertips. She raised her eyes to his face and whispered, "Why'd you blow me off at lunch?"

"I realized I had stuff to do." His dark eyes shifted to the hand he was running through her hair.

You didn't have to be a homicide detective to spot that tell. The lie was so obvious, Denver didn't even try to cover it.

She didn't need honesty right now. She'd never demanded that much from the men in her life anyway. Stroking his cheek, she said, "Kiss me."

The fingers sifting through her hair wove around the strands and he pulled her closer. When their lips met, she tasted peppermint and possibilities.

His hand slid to the back of her head and he broke their connection. "I don't want you hurting your neck—even for a kiss."

"If you can't risk it all for a hot kiss, there's something missing in your soul." She touched his bottom lip with the pad of her thumb. "I forgot all about my whiplash for a minute."

"Let me help you forget some more." He wrapped his hands around her waist and pulled her into his lap. Her dress rode up her thigh, and he ran his rough palm across its curve.

"I don't know how you could've believed you were flying beneath the radar at that party in this dress."

She burrowed into his lap and hung an arm around his neck. "I was a moth among butterflies. Believe me. The flash and glitz in that room could've blinded you."

"That's why you probably stood out. You don't need flash and glitz. You have something more indefinable than that—style, sexiness without hitting people in the face with it."

She must be her mother's daughter after all. "Can we stop talking now? I thought you were the strong, silent type."

He gently took her face between his hands and kissed her mouth, his tongue slipping between her lips. She'd wanted him from the moment she'd seen him at the lake, but she always did go after the unattainable ones.

As she peeled herself from his chest, she whispered against his lips, "Let's take this to my bedroom."

His dark eyes searched her face. "Are you sure?"

"My neck is fine."

"I wasn't talking about your neck, I—"

She knew exactly what he meant, but the ring

from her phone cut him off. She held up her finger. "Normally, I wouldn't take a call at a moment like this, but under the circumstances…"

Rolling from his lap, she grabbed her phone from the coffee table. She held it in front of him. "It's Lulu."

"Take it."

"Hi, Lulu." She carefully pressed the button for the speaker.

"Girl, are you all right?"

"Why wouldn't I be all right?" The blood thumped in her ears.

"You bounced out of here so fast I thought maybe someone recognized you."

"Recognized me? I thought you said it was okay for me to be there."

"Cut the crap, Ashlynn. I know who you are and, if anyone else does, you could be in big trouble."

Chapter Twelve

Ashlynn licked her lips and flicked a quick glance at Denver, who avoided giving her the *I told you so* look. "Do you think anyone else knows?"

"I'm not sure, but that's not the point. I've been reading the blog, so I know what you're after. I don't know who killed Tiana Fuller, but I do know for a fact that she was working for my sister's campaign. That cop will never find her name on any paperwork here, but I've got proof…if you want it."

"I do want it." Ashlynn rubbed the back of her neck. "Can you email or text it to me?"

Lulu paused. "I wouldn't chance it. Meet me tonight and I'll hand over the proof."

Denver jabbed her hip and shook his head.

She rolled her eyes at him. "How about tomorrow?"

"I want to unload this as soon as possible. I stole it, and I don't want it in my possession anymore. Come get it tonight, or I'm tossing it."

"Wait, wait. I'll meet you. Tell me where." She pointed to Denver and then herself. He could come along. In fact, she wanted him at least in the vicinity.

Lulu said, "There's a dog park at Mulholland and Laurel Canyon. I'll meet you in the parking lot in an hour."

Ashlynn ignored Denver's furious slicing motions in the air and answered Lulu. "I'll be there. It's going to be safe, right?"

"You don't have to worry about me. I want to help you, but nobody can know what I'm doing. I didn't make you fill out that paperwork today, did I? That's because I recognized you right away. I just wanna be part of the blog."

"I'm not going to call you out."

"God, no. Don't do that, but I'd still know I was part of the blog."

"Okay. I'll see you in an hour."

When she ended the call, she held up her hand against Denver's protests. "She's right. She kept quiet about me today at the campaign headquarters when she could've outed me, and she invited me to the fundraiser, knowing who I was."

"You don't even know if she's telling the truth. Maybe she had no idea who you were earlier. She just found out at the fundraiser because someone told her, and now she'd luring you out with promises of proof that Tiana worked for the campaign." He sat forward and grabbed her hands. "Someone just tried to bulldoze you off Mulholland and now you're returning to…Mulholland. Not a great idea."

"You're coming with me." She drilled her finger into his chest, regretting she'd never even gotten to take off his shirt.

He captured her finger. "This time. I can't be protecting you twenty-four seven, Ashlynn. I do have a job."

"I don't need protection all day, every day. This is one situation that might be a little sketchy, and this *is* your job."

He squeezed his eyes closed and pinched the bridge of his nose. "If Lulu has this proof that Tiana worked for her sister, why not just call me?"

"You're kidding, right? If Veronica Escalante or her top dog, Jed, knew Lulu even had this information, never mind turning it over to the cops, they'd go ballistic."

"Why? Why the secrecy?" He slammed his fist into his palm. "If they didn't have anything to hide, why would it matter that Tiana worked for the campaign? They must be involved in her death or know something about it."

"Or they just don't want the campaign to be associated with a murder." She pushed up from the couch, tugging on the hem of her dress. "I'm going to change for this meeting. It's probably better if she doesn't see you. She'd recognize you, anyway."

"You think?" He pinched the material of his cotton T-shirt between his fingers. "I'm not wearing my suit, and I have a baseball cap in the car."

"Oh, she noticed you today. I doubt she's going to forget what you look like, regardless of your clothes." She headed for her bedroom and spun around. "Dodgers, Angels or Padres?"

"What?" He glanced up from his phone, his brows knitted over his nose.

"The baseball cap—Dodgers, Angels or Padres?"

"Are you serious? The Dodgers, of course."

She nodded and slipped into her bedroom.

"LULU HAD BETTER not be here early. One look at me and she'll probably bolt—if what you said was true and she'd recognize me." The knots in Denver's gut tightened as he took the last curve toward the dog park.

"Lulu thought you were hot. She's not going to forget." Ashlynn glanced at the phone in her hand. "Besides, we got here in thirty-five minutes. There's no way she'd be this early."

"If Lulu's not alone, take off."

"And leave you out in the park?"

"You can swing by and pick me up later. Get out of here if something feels off." His hands gripping the steering wheel, Denver turned into the lot for the park.

It was really a playground for kids, with equipment and everything, but it was also an off-leash dog park for part of the day. The edge of the common area rushed downhill in a tangle of bushes and undergrowth. He didn't want to hide that far away from the car. He didn't want to be here at all. When people had to meet in secret to give up information they shouldn't have, it all screamed danger.

He let out a long breath as he scanned the empty

parking lot. A few lights beamed down on the asphalt, and Denver pulled in under one of them.

He cracked open the driver's-side door. "You could leave the engine running, just in case you need to make a quick getaway. If you see any other car besides Lulu's BMW pull in, take off. If you see anyone in her passenger seat, take off."

"I got it, Denver." She pushed at his arm. "You'd better find your hiding spot before Lulu gets here. She might take off herself if she sees you."

"I'll be behind that clump of bushes at the edge of the playground. If worse comes to worst, run toward me and I'll have you covered."

"You mean with a gun?"

He patted his hip where he'd clipped his holster back onto his belt at her place. "Yeah."

"And I've got my pepper spray." She pulled her purse into her lap.

"Then we've got all bases covered." He tugged on a lock of her hair. "Be careful, and don't do anything stupid."

"I'll be fine. Go."

He stepped from the car, and Ashlynn didn't even bother getting out on her side. He watched through the window as she crawled over the console and slid into the driver's seat.

He loped toward the swing set and ducked behind the bushes bordering the play area. He crouched on his haunches and played with the branches of the bush to get a clear view of his car and Ashlynn's silhouette.

That phone call from Lulu had saved him from making a big mistake tonight. As much as he wanted Ashlynn, he didn't need the emotional entanglement right now—or ever. Would he be crouching behind a bush in the middle of the night if they hadn't almost wound up in her bed?

He sucked in a breath as a pair of headlights swept into the parking lot. Squinting into the darkness, he made out the BMW logo on the front of the car, but he couldn't tell who was driving or if the driver had company.

The car pulled into a space two down from Ashlynn, and the dome light illuminated the interior as the driver got out of the vehicle. His muscles relaxed a little when he recognized Lulu, tossing her long dark hair over her shoulder. She obviously hadn't changed from the party, and the light from the lamp above caught the sequins on her dress, which shimmered as she approached Ashlynn.

As Ashlynn popped her own door, Denver murmured to himself, "No, no, no. Stay in the car."

The two women met in the parking lot, and he strained to hear their voices, rising and falling in a conversational cadence. He covered his mouth with his hand and said, "Get the proof and get out."

As Denver massaged a cramp in his thigh, he caught sight of a shadow moving into the parking lot from the road. His nostrils flared. Was that an animal? Coyotes and even mountain lions roamed this area. The park had closed for a while a few years ago after a coyote had attacked a few dogs.

He blinked at the spot where he'd noticed the movement. The shadow had taken the shape of a dark figure—a man-sized figure. Denver grabbed his gun from the holster, the muscles in his legs coiled.

People came to this park all the time at night for a variety of reasons, but they usually drove cars. A walk from one of the nearby residences would be a tricky proposition, and it was a bit late for a stroll.

Had Ashlynn and Lulu noticed the man? Denver whistled in what he hoped was an approximation of a night bird's cry. He didn't even care at this point if Lulu made him.

Ashlynn turned her head to the side.

Had she noticed the man yet?

Lulu had. She jerked back and grabbed Ashlynn's arm as the man emerged from the shadows, his arm outstretched as he approached them.

The light glinted on an object in the stranger's hand and his voice carried all the way to the playground. "Hand it over."

Gripping his weapon, Denver lunged from his hiding place. "Get down, get down, get down."

The adrenaline coursing through his veins propelled him into the parking lot.

Ashlynn dropped to the ground and grabbed Lulu's hand, dragging her down with her.

The man spun around and ran for the edge of the park, speeding across the grass flattened by countless dogs over the years.

Denver gave chase, shouting over his shoulder, "Get in the car and leave—now."

He slammed into the side of a picnic table that had come out of nowhere, his knees hitting the attached bench, his palms slapping the top of the table. Cursing, he pushed off and scanned the edge of the canyon that dipped away from the park.

The man had disappeared into the foliage. Had probably rolled down the hill. Denver didn't want to play hide-and-seek in the canyon, even if he had the superior weapon.

He gave up the chase and limped back to the parking lot, the gun still in his hand. This guy could have an accomplice.

He tripped to a stop, his heart thundering in his chest. Lulu's BMW was gone, but his car sat in the same spot…empty. He'd told Ashlynn to get in the car and take off, but maybe someone had prevented her from leaving.

The breath rasped in his throat as he yelled, "Ashlynn! Ashlynn!"

A head popped up on the driver's side of the car, and he stumbled again, his knees weak. He circled around the vehicle and yanked on the handle of the passenger side. The locks clicked and he tried again, swinging the door open so hard it almost closed again.

He dropped onto the seat and asked, "Are you okay?"

"I'm fine. What happened out there?"

"Move." He smacked the dashboard with his hand. "Move."

She cranked on the engine and peeled out of the parking lot, the back tires fishtailing on the loose dirt.

When she steadied the car, he smoothed a hand over her arm. "What happened? Is Lulu all right?"

"She's okay, but she's not happy with me."

"With you? Is she the one who invited the goon with the knife to the meeting?"

"If she was, she's a good actress. She was as surprised and scared as I was when he showed up."

"What did he want? What did he say? I heard 'hand it over' at about the same time I saw the glint of the knife in his hand."

"H-he said he wanted our phones, cash, jewelry."

Denver said, "He was pretending to be a common mugger, but we know better, and Lulu knows better. The whole thing could've been a setup, designed to lure you into another dangerous situation."

"I don't think so, Denver. I don't think Lulu knew about the man with the knife."

"Really? She gets you to meet her at a deserted park in the dead of night on the pretense of giving you proof that Tiana worked for the Escalante campaign and, instead of getting the proof, you almost get knifed. And *she's* mad at *you*?" He plowed a hand through his hair.

"But it didn't play out like that."

"What do you mean? I saw it unfold right in front of me. I chased the guy before he disappeared into the canyon."

"Yeah, that all happened, but I didn't walk away empty-handed." Ashlynn reached into the cup holder and dangled a thumb drive from her fingertips. "Lulu delivered the goods."

Chapter Thirteen

Denver jerked his head to the side, almost giving himself whiplash. He held out his hand and she dropped the thumb drive onto his palm. "Did she say what was on it?"

"Nope." Ashlynn carefully negotiated the last curve and pulled up to a red light at the bottom of the hill. "Just told me it contained proof that Tiana worked for the Escalante campaign."

"How'd she get a copy? They must know she has it."

"Slow down a minute." Ashlynn rubbed the back of her neck. "I can't drive, talk and think at the same time, not when I can't even turn my head."

"Take the turn onto Hollywood Boulevard. We'll get coffee. I have a lot of questions for you."

She slid a gaze to the side. "I have a few for you, too. Why are you limping?"

"I tripped over a picnic bench in the dark. Once that happened, your assailant had disappeared into the canyon that borders the park. I had no chance of finding him." He tapped on the windshield. "Pull into that diner."

Ashlynn signaled a left turn and cruised into the lot of an all-night diner. Patrons for the nearby clubs and bars packed the place, and they grabbed a table in the corner that hadn't been cleared yet.

A busboy swept up the clutter as they sat and ordered two coffees.

Denver, having pocketed the thumb drive, drew it out and dangled it over the table by its ribbon. "This is the proof, huh?"

"That's what Lulu said—before we were rudely interrupted."

"Lulu seemed surprised by the intrusion?"

"Surprised, scared, mad. It was legit. She didn't know." Ashlynn spread her hands on the table, her thumbs touching. "Besides, why would she hand off evidence to me while she was planning to have someone take it right away?"

"To cover herself." He bobbled the drive. "We don't yet know what this contains. It could be garbage."

"One way to find out. Don't know why we're wasting our time here." She circled her finger in the air.

He closed his hand around the device. "Because you—we both just had a scare. The information on this thumb drive isn't going anywhere."

The waitress came to their table and poured coffee into their upturned cups. "Anything else?"

Denver asked, "Do you have blueberry pie?"

"We do, hon. Ice cream with that?"

"Ice cream and two forks." Denver held up two fingers.

Cupping her chin with her hand, Ashlynn tilted her head. "I thought most cops dealt with stress by drinking whiskey. Your poison is blueberry pie à la mode?"

He blew on his coffee before taking a sip. "Don't knock it until you've tried it. A lot of people eat when they're stressed out."

"Or don't."

"Sorry?"

"Never mind." She rubbed her hands together. "I'm ready for your questions. I'm anxious to see what we have here."

"What were you and Lulu talking about for so long? I thought you'd grab whatever she had and we'd get out of there."

"I wanted to ask her how she knew who I was."

"And?"

"She's a big fan of the blog—was a big fan of my brother's."

Denver trapped his sigh in his throat. Couldn't she just once take credit for the blog without bringing her brother into it?

"You said before, your picture's not on the blog and you keep a low profile otherwise. How'd she know you were Ashlynn Hughes?"

"Just my luck, she's kind of obsessive about true crime in general and *LA Confidential* in particular." She folded her hands around her cup and stared into the steam rising from it. "When Sean was murdered,

Lulu followed everything about the case and, somewhere in the coverage, my name was mentioned. She looked me up. She saw my picture and recognized me that first day. That's why she didn't follow up with Jed's instructions to have me fill out paperwork, which would've meant a copy of my driver's license."

"You dodged a bullet. Is that why she didn't turn you in to Jed? Because she's a super fan of the blog?"

"That's one reason, or maybe it's the main reason. She invited me to the fundraiser and offered me this info because she wants to be involved in the blog."

"Why didn't she just give you the proof tonight at the party?"

She crinkled her nose. "She wasn't sure she was going to turn it over. Then when I left so suddenly, she thought I might be in trouble and figured she needed to reveal the truth. She swears neither Jed nor Veronica knows my identity."

"Someone does." He smacked his fist on the table, sending tiny ripples through the coffee.

"Does that mean you want more coffee?" The waitress delivered the pie, two scoops of vanilla ice cream already melting into the crust."

"Sorry, just making a point. This looks great, thanks." Denver aimed a smile at the waitress. He didn't want her to think he and Ashlynn were fighting.

She glanced at Ashlynn's full cup. "Do you want something else, hon?"

"Water would be great."

Denver plucked a couple of paper napkins from

the dispenser on the table and dropped them onto his lap. He pointed his fork at Ashlynn. "You'd better eat some of this pie, or that waitress is going to think this is some kind of domestic situation."

"Only a cop would think something like that." She plucked up a fork and ran the tines through the ice cream, scooping up a berry from the plate.

The tart berries exploded in his mouth as the sweet ice cream melted down his throat. He closed his eyes, and Ashlynn nudged his foot under the table.

"Earth to Denver."

"See? Just relaxing." He swiped a napkin across his mouth. "When the stranger approached you, did Lulu seem to recognize him? Did you?"

"He was wearing a ski mask." She asked, "You didn't notice that?"

"I never got a good look at his face He stayed out of the light. How about his voice? Did it sound familiar?"

"No. Didn't jolt any memories for me." She held up her hand. "And before you ask me about race, hair color or anything like that, I couldn't tell you. He had a black turtleneck that met the ski mask, jeans, black gloves. All I can tell you is that he was average height because he was about as tall as me and a little shorter than you."

"Great." He dug his fork into the pie. "And he was a fast runner."

"Are you done with your questions?" She pulled

her phone from her purse. "I'm going to check on Lulu."

"Not yet. We need to look at what's on the thumb drive first. If it's junk, she set you up. You need to know that before you communicate with her again." He picked up the other fork, lopped off a piece of pie and held it in front of her lips. "Try it. I can't eat the whole thing."

"Looks like you're doing a great job." She eyed the pie as if it were going to bite her instead of the other way around.

He tipped the fork back and forth. "Going, going..."

Ashlynn opened her mouth and closed her lips around the fork. She chewed for a few seconds and said, "Gone."

He pointed his fork at her phone on the table. "Lulu didn't text you, did she?"

"She didn't. When she heard you shouting, her eyes shot daggers at me. She hadn't expected me to bring company, even if she didn't recognize you as the hot cop from before."

"Even though I could've been saving your lives at that point? What did she think was going to happen? What did you think was going happen?"

"I figured we'd hand over our money, phones, jewelry, and then he'd ask me for the thumb drive, like, 'by the way, give me that, too,' even though we'd all know that's what he'd wanted in the first place."

"He could've hurt you. He had a knife. That's no joke. Yeah, it wasn't a match for my gun, but when someone is that close to you, a knife can do fatal damage."

"I'd transferred my pepper spray from my purse to my pocket. Before you stormed out of your hiding place, I'd planned on using it."

Denver's heart skipped several beats. That could've been a deadly move on Ashlynn's part. He opened his mouth and then nipped it shut. She hadn't had to use the pepper spray—no point in lecturing her.

He pushed away the plate, which had become a swirling mess of purple and white. "We know we weren't followed to the park. I made sure of it on the way over. The only way that guy shows up is if the meeting was a setup, or he followed Lulu."

"He followed Lulu. There's no way that was a setup, or Lulu should stop wasting her time stuffing envelopes and become an actress. She was clearly shocked." Ashlynn ran the tip of her finger through the blueberry swirl and sucked it off.

Denver followed the action and swallowed a gulp of lukewarm coffee. "Why is Lulu being followed? Is it because Jed or her sister don't trust her, or is it because someone saw her talking to you and knows she invited you to the gala?"

"I don't know. Did the pie do its job? Are you done unwinding?" She fingered the thumb drive he'd left on the table. "I'm dying to find out what's on this thing."

"That—" he slipped the drive into his pocket and slapped a ten on the table "—is a bad choice of words."

HE'D TAKEN OVER the driving duty from Ashlynn and forty minutes later, he pulled into the driveway of her duplex.

As they'd turned onto her block, Denver had driven slowly and studied every car. Maybe they hadn't been followed, but the people after Ashlynn had already proved they knew where she lived. A few new locks might not be enough to keep them out, especially if they believed she had proof that Tiana had volunteered for the campaign in her possession.

When he put the car in Park, he reached for her arm. "Do me a favor and sit in the car until I come around and let you out."

"Is this a sudden spasm of chivalry, or do you think someone's watching us?"

"Chivalry all day, baby."

"Right." She smirked but stayed put as he hustled around to her side, his hand hovering over his gun.

He cracked open the door. "Okay, let's move"

Luckily, Ashlynn's long legs kept up with his stride as he propelled her to the front door. While she unlocked the dead bolt, he did a half turn and blocked her body with his, his gaze scanning the sidewalk and probing the bushes.

He followed her inside and locked up as she headed straight for her laptop.

"You finally ready to see what we have here?"

"Sated with blueberry pie and ready." He pulled the thumb drive from his pocket and handed it to her.

When she woke up her computer, she inserted the drive into the port on the side. A folder opened, containing a video from a phone. Ashlynn double clicked on it.

When the video launched, it displayed a blurry thumbnail of the side of a desk.

"Play it." Denver said the words at the same time Ashlynn clicked the play button.

They both huddled forward to watch, their heads almost touching.

A man's voice came over the computer's speakers as the video showed a table with a couple of cans of soda and a woman's arm, her fingers tapping the table. "So, you're good with that, Tiana?"

Ashlynn sucked in a breath. "That's Jed's voice."

A female voice responded. "Sure. I'll do whatever it takes to stop a second term for Mayor Wexler."

Jed said, "Hold on. I need to answer this text."

The view of the camera shifted upward as Jed held up the phone, pretending to answer a text. As Tiana Fuller came into focus, Denver said, "Stop it."

Ashlynn clicked the mouse. "Tiana doesn't know she's being filmed, does she? Jed was holding the phone in his hand and secretly turned on the video. Now he's pretending to answer a text just so he can hold up the phone and capture Tiana on camera."

"Exactly." Denver's jaw tightened as he looked at Tiana, vibrant and very much alive. "Let's hope Jed reiterates what he just suggested to Tiana, and what she just agreed to do."

When Ashlynn tapped Play, Tiana came to life and tucked a strand of light brown hair behind her ear, presumably waiting for Jed to stop texting.

The camera view shifted to the side, as if Jed were still holding it up but not pointing it directly at Tiana. Jed continued. "It's just a few dirty tricks, right? Nothing too serious, nothing against the law. Campaigns do it all the time. Hell, we might have a Wexler mole in our own office."

Tiana laughed; a high, tinkling sound that made Denver flinch. "You never know, huh? This could be fun. This is the side of politics that interests me— the behind-the-scenes stuff, what makes a campaign tick."

"I'm with you on that. The upside is that Veronica Escalante is a great leader. You'll be providing a great service to the city if you can help get her elected as the next mayor of LA."

"I can't wait to start. Will you invite me to all the war room meetings? I feel as if I have a lot to learn from you, Mr. Gordon. You're the best." Tiana gave a flirtatious giggle.

Jed coughed. "I think I can teach you a few tricks."

The video ended and Ashlyn turned to face Denver, her eyes wide. "Sounds like Jed recruited Tiana to spy on the Wexler campaign. Why would he lie to you about knowing her, and why'd he take this video?"

"I'm not sure about any of that yet, but after watching that video—" he tapped the laptop's screen "—I'm starting to wonder who was playing who."

Chapter Fourteen

"Something sounded off to me, too." Ashlynn sat back and jabbed a finger at the video still on the screen. "Was Tiana *flirting* with Jed? He sounded all in control, and then she turned on the feminine charm to flatter him when she didn't need to. She'd already gotten the gig, right? Sounds like she'd got it even before the video started."

"I'm glad you heard it, too. I didn't know if I was picking up on her tone because I'm a guy or because I'm a detective. But the dynamic shifted at the end." He shoved that lock of hair from his forehead. "One thing that is clear from this video is that the Escalante campaign was using Tiana to get some dirt on the Wexler campaign."

Ashlynn bit the side of her thumb. "Maybe she got the dirt, someone from the CREW found out and killed her for it."

"Why would the Escalante campaign be hiding that information?" He spread his hands. "If Jed's right and everyone plays these tricks, what's the problem for them? I'd say murder is a little more serious than campaign dirty tricks. You'd think he'd want to point the finger at the Wexler campaign."

"You'd think. I mean that's not a good look for Escalante, either. Set up a young girl to pull a fast one on a political campaign, and then she gets murdered."

"Why?" Denver jumped up from the couch and circled the room. "What exactly did Tiana find out about Wexler? And if she did dig up some serious infraction, why wouldn't Escalante use it? That info should be all over the news by now."

Ashlynn flopped back against the cushions of the couch, suddenly exhausted. "Something's not adding up, but I guess it explains why Tiana never told her parents she was working for Escalante. She must've been there in an undercover capacity. That's why the other volunteers didn't know her—and I believe them."

"Lulu knew about Tiana because Lulu, whether she likes it or not, is in the inner circle. Maybe that's why Lulu gave you the video. She thinks it's going to help her sister's campaign." Denver finally stopped pacing and propped his shoulder against the wall, folding his arms.

"I'm not sure Lulu is all that interested in helping her sister's campaign, but I'm wondering why she decided to color outside the lines and copy this video. Just to be part of *LA Confidential*?"

"And why did Jed make the video?"

"That makes no sense to me, either." She patted the couch next to her. "Have a seat. You're making me nervous, and you're still limping."

"Maybe he made it to have proof that Tiana agreed to the spying, in case things went sideways and she accused the campaign of coercing her." Denver sliced his hand through the air, still standing against the wall. "That doesn't make sense. Jed still looks complicit in that video. He's not doing himself any favors."

"Maybe he didn't make the video for protection but as proof he asked Tiana. Maybe he made the video for Veronica."

Denver shrugged and then crossed the room to perch on the arm of the couch, his leg brushing her arm. "Whatever his motives, Lulu got hold of the video and gave it to you."

"Speaking of Lulu, now that we know her proof was legit, I'm going to text her and make sure she's okay."

Denver warned. "Keep me out of it. Even if she thinks she recognized me, don't cop to it—and tell her to be careful. She has an enemy in the campaign."

Ashlynn snatched up her phone from next to the computer on the coffee table, and typed a message to Lulu. She waved the phone at Denver. "I just told her thanks for the video and asked if she was okay."

"How about you?" He stroked her hair. "Are you okay? The threats seem to be building against you—two in one day. How's your neck?"

She squeezed the back of her neck. "The car wreck seems like it happened days ago. I feel all right. Did you happen to hear from the tow service about my car?"

He patted his pocket. "Forgot to tell you. They towed the car and tested it at the yard. It started just fine. I can take you there tomorrow morning to pick it up. They mentioned a few scratches on the body and sent pictures. I'll send those to you."

"Now I'm feeling even better."

He asked, "Anything from Lulu yet?"

"No. My phone dings when texts come through." She turned over her phone and glanced at the display, just in case. "I hope she's okay, too. She must've risked a lot to get that video and then hand it off to me."

"What is it with Lulu, anyway? Does she hate or love her sister?"

"A little of both, I think." Ashlynn picked up her laptop and carried it to her kitchen table. She plugged in the charger. "She doesn't like the phoniness of politicians, but Veronica basically supports Lulu in a style that she enjoys—mostly from Veronica's husband."

"I looked him up. The dude's a high roller. He's putting up buildings all over downtown LA. Even if Escalante loses, and I think she will, she won't be hurting for money."

Ashlynn ran her fingers through her hair. "I'm glad you were there tonight. I don't know if that guy would've hurt us, but he would've taken the thumb drive for sure."

"I wasn't about to let you meet Lulu on your own, not after what happened on Mulholland." He rubbed his knee. "Even if I missed the guy."

"Maybe *you* need some ice." She tipped her head toward the fridge. "Can I get you some?"

"I'll survive, but you can give me the thumb drive."

She dropped her lashes and wound an errant strand of hair around her finger. "You're leaving already?"

"Already? It's late. I thought you were exhausted." He stretched, and her gaze meandered down his body.

"I thought maybe…before…" She covered her warm face with her hands. "I was hoping you'd stay, and we could finish what we'd started earlier, before Lulu's text."

The silence from across the room rolled over her in waves. She spread open her fingers and peered at him through the narrow spaces.

He rose slowly from the couch, as if in slow motion, his gait halting, which had nothing to do with his knee.

His eyes kindled with a dark seductiveness that she felt as a tremble through her body. Her toes curled into the floor.

"You're sure?" His voice sounded gruff, as if he hadn't used it in years. Or maybe there was something else he hadn't used in years.

"You don't want me to sign a contract, do you?" Without expending conscious effort in the act, she'd been moving toward him and the invitation in his eyes.

"No, but—" he spread his hands "—I don't have any protection."

She flicked her fingers. "I do."

At the quirk of his eyebrows, she said, "I—I mean they're leftovers. Could even be expired by now."

His lips curled, and they were close enough now that she could see the slight flush on his throat. "I'm willing to take my chances, if you are."

She exhaled, and he took the final step toward her and gathered her into his arms. His kiss burned hotter than it had before, as if he'd been warming up and now it was full-steam ahead.

She wrapped her arms around his neck and sagged against his body. She didn't have the energy to play any games with him. If he could take her right now, she'd gladly face her next brush with death.

As if he sensed she'd never let him go, he swept her up into his arms and murmured against her lips, "Bedroom?"

"Uh-huh." Her place was small enough that he remembered the way, and her body jostled against his as he carried her to her room.

He actually had to kick open the door, which only added to the deliciousness of this moment. His next move had to be tossing her across the bed, but he must've figured her body had endured too much trauma tonight.

He backed up to the bed and sat on the edge, still holding her, folding her into his lap, her long legs awkwardly hanging over his thighs, her toes brushing the carpet.

She ran her hands beneath his shirt, the texture of his warm skin causing her fingertips to buzz. Lulu could keep her smooth sugar daddy. She'd take this slightly tangy, rough-around-the-edges cop any day.

Denver fell back on the bed and toed off his shoes.

Rolling to his side, she yanked open the drawer of her nightstand, feeling around for the foil packets of condoms.

She dragged out a strip and waved them in the air. "I think they're still good."

He unbuckled his belt and unzipped his jeans. "I think they have a shelf life of a hundred years, just in case."

She curled her hand over his as he hooked a thumb in his fly. "Let me undress you a little at a time. I'm not sure my system can withstand the shock of seeing a totally naked man in my bed all at once."

"Watch what you're calling little."

She giggled like a virgin schoolgirl and tugged at his shirt. As it rolled up his body, her hands replaced the material and she caressed his flesh, feeling him shiver beneath her touch.

She planted a kiss at the base of his throat where his pulse throbbed and slid her hand down his belly to his open fly. She peeled back his jeans and he lifted his hips to help her do the honors.

Suddenly, she lost all patience, hooked her thumbs beneath the elastic of his boxers and yanked them down to his muscular thighs along with his jeans.

She sighed and smoothed her hands over him. "Nothing little about it."

He kicked off his pants. "Your turn and, unlike you, I'm looking forward to seeing a totally naked woman all at once. I'll get over the shock quick enough."

She unbuttoned her shirt and shrugged out of it. Presenting her back to him, she said, "Can you unhook my bra? It sort of hurts my neck when I reach around."

With a twist of his fingers, he unhooked her and didn't even wait for the bra to come off her arms before he reached around and cupped her breasts.

He sucked in a breath. "Pretty and pert, just as I'd imagined them."

She cranked her head over her shoulder despite the pain. "You were imagining my breasts."

"Among other things." He stroked her cheek. "Turn around."

She shimmied around to face him and then lay on the bed next to him. He pulled off her jeans and underwear as she twisted this way and that—anything to facilitate his access to her body.

He trailed his fingers from her neck to her belly, and she arched her back. Placing a finger against her throbbing lips, he said, "Don't hurt your neck. I'll do all the work."

She narrowed her eyes. "Do you think making love to me is going to be work?"

"Some of us love our jobs."

And she approved of the tools of his trade as he used his lips, tongue and fingers to push all the right buttons.

When he had her breathless and panting, he entered her fully.

Her hands clawed through his thick hair and then she dug her fingernails into his shoulders as he moved against her, in her, with her. Her muscles tightened, and she wrapped her arms and legs around his frame, drawing him further inside.

Ashlynn broke apart when she reached her climax, which gave him the signal to release. As she came down from her high, he thrust into her, building to his own peak.

When he came inside her, she felt his pleasure in every shiver and tremble of his body. Spent, he shifted to her side and growled in her ear, "Was that worth all the pain and suffering you've been through?"

Speechless, she nodded and turned toward him, molding her body to his side.

When the lethargy left her body and Denver's breathing no longer sounded like he'd just run a marathon, Ashlynn scooted off the bed. "I'm going to brush my teeth and splash some water on my face."

"I'll dispose of the evidence and put some toothpaste on my finger and run it across my teeth." He gathered up the used condom with a tissue from her nightstand and planted his feet on the floor.

"I may even have an extra toothbrush from my dentist, so you don't need to rough it."

As Denver went to the kitchen to get some water, Ashlynn brushed her teeth, washed her face and found a brand-new toothbrush for him.

He handed her a glass of water and disappeared

into the bathroom. By the time he came out, she'd straightened the covers and fluffed the pillows.

"Come join me." She patted the bed. "This is the part where we cuddle. Do you mind?"

"If that means I get to relish the touch of your bare skin against mine and wrap my fingers in your red-gold hair as I drift off to sleep, you can call that anything you like."

The bed dipped as he slid in beside her. He hadn't been kidding about the skin-on-skin contact or the hair, but there was no drifting for Denver. Within minutes of his head hitting the pillow, he was out.

She soaked in the feel of his heavy arm around her waist, his warm breath against the back of her neck. It felt good to have someone on that side of the bed again—she'd even deal with the messed-up covers in the morning.

He took a few shuddering breaths and rolled away from her, onto his other side.

A few minutes later, she hoisted herself up on one elbow and peered over his shoulder. That pesky lock of hair lay plastered against his forehead. Lifting it with one finger, she kissed the skin beneath it, her breasts pressing against his arm.

He stirred and mumbled in his sleep, and she held her breath until he settled again, his breathing slow and steady.

Then she slipped out of the bed. She bent at the waist and picked up his T-shirt from the floor, pinching it between two fingers. Dangling the shirt by her side, she tiptoed from the bedroom. She pulled the door almost closed behind her.

She dragged his T-shirt over her head, thrusting her hands through the sleeves. Her nostrils flared as she inhaled his scent—a mixture of citrus and spicy, his body wash and deodorant at war with each other.

With the T-shirt brushing her thighs, she padded to the kitchen, the cold tile shocking the soles of her bare feet. She settled into a chair at the kitchen table, and flipped open her charging laptop, the thumb drive still jutting out from the side.

She right-clicked the video icon on the screen and made quick work of copying the recording to her laptop. She ejected the drive and tugged it from the computer port. Swinging the thumb drive from its ribbon, she crept to where Denver had left his jacket draped over the back of the chair and tucked it into his pocket—so he wouldn't forget it in the morning.

She returned to the laptop, eyeing it as if it were a dangerous snake ready to strike. Then she plopped down on the chair and brought up *LA Confidential*.

Biting her bottom lip, she glanced down the hallway at the bedroom door behind which Denver lay slumbering like a man with no reason to suspect a betrayal. She shook her head and brushed her hair out of her face. Denver hadn't told her *not* to post this video.

The people of LA had a right to know the dirt about the campaign of one of its mayoral candidates. Her online sleuths had a right to know. Maybe with this video out there, someone else might step forward with more information. As far as Ashlynn could tell, her readers were the ones bringing the heat on this investigation—not the LAPD.

She clicked on the button for a new post and began to type, the words of the blockbuster story pounding against her temples. She read the first few sentences aloud in a harsh whisper. "'Escalante campaign busted. Proof surfaces that murdered student Tiana Fuller had volunteered for the campaign in a covert role.'"

Ashlynn's fingers flew across the keyboard, each click a nail in the coffin of her budding relationship with Detective Denver Holt.

Chapter Fifteen

Denver woke up with a start, his body bolting upright in the bed. For a second, he couldn't remember where he was. Then his fingers smoothed a lock of Ashlynn's bright hair against her pillow. But he sure remembered who he was with.

He eased out of the bed and crept from the room on silent feet. Ashlynn seemed to have a well-stocked fridge, unlike most single women he knew, so maybe he could whip up some breakfast for them before they had to take off.

He couldn't let her sleep much longer. He had to get home and change before work, and drop off Ashlynn at the tow yard to pick up her car. He couldn't exactly go into the station looking like this.

He swept his boxers from the floor and stepped into them. Then he snatched his neatly folded T-shirt from the top of her dresser. He cocked his head as he shook out the shirt. Had he placed it there while in the throes of lust? If so, he'd exercised more self-control than he remembered. He shrugged and pulled it over his head. After tugging up his jeans, he made a beeline for the kitchen.

Ashlynn's laptop sat on the kitchen table, charging. His heart skipped a beat as he brushed his hand across the side of the computer where he'd expected to find the thumb drive sticking out.

Then his heart skipped another beat as Ashlynn stood, framed in the hallway, naked from her head to her toes, a grin lighting up her face. "Good morning."

"Morning, you." He jabbed a finger at the laptop. "I was looking for Lulu's thumb drive."

"I put it in your pocket, so you wouldn't forget it this morning." She stretched her arms over her head, tangling her hair in her fingers, just as he'd done last night. "Are you making breakfast, or what?"

He made a sweeping motion with his hand. "Go do your thing. I'll whip up something."

While Ashlynn showered and dressed, Denver scrambled some eggs and shoved a couple of pieces of bread in the toaster. She'd run out of coffee, but he could always drink the swill at the station.

He glanced at her closed laptop on the table. She was usually glued to that thing first thing in the morning. Shower must've been more important than the blog this morning.

"Smells great." She bustled through the room, her long legs in a pair of dark jeans, her red hair vibrant against an emerald-green sweater. She joined him in the kitchen. "Sorry, I don't have any coffee. Tea?"

"I'll get some coffee at the station." He nodded at

her plate on the table and jabbed a fork into his own eggs. "I forgot to tell you yesterday in all the excitement, Tiana's parents mentioned a boy. A young man Tiana was hanging out with ever since the beginning of the new semester. They figured he lived nearby because she saw him when she was home."

"You already told me about him. Tony Fuentes, right?"

"Good memory. I must still be rattled." He shook his head as if to clear it, but he didn't think he'd ever dismiss the memory of Ashlynn's body beneath his hands. "With any luck, we'll get his number from Tiana's phone records. Weird that he hasn't called us if he was that close to Tiana."

"If he was her boyfriend, it's strange that he hasn't stepped forward." She crunched her toast.

"Not sure it reached that level, but parents are usually the last to know with these new dating rules."

"Are there new rules?" She blinked. "No wonder I can't get lucky."

He cleared his throat. "What would you call last night?"

"Luck had nothing to do with that." She fluttered her eyelashes. "I set my sights on you from the start."

Had she? Instead of feeling flattered, wings of anxiety took flight in his belly. He'd stumbled right into her web by playing the hero to the rescue. She'd been in real danger, though. She hadn't faked any of that.

She nudged him. "I'm joking."

"We'd better get moving." He shoved the last bite

of toast in his mouth and chewed. "After I drop you at the tow yard, I have to go home and shower and change." He took his plate to the sink and rinsed it off before putting it in the dishwasher. "The thumb drive is in my pocket, right?"

"Yeah." She bumped his hip with hers in front of the sink. "I'm going to finish these delicious eggs, and then I'll put away the rest of this stuff. You should collect your gun. You don't wanna leave that here."

He tugged at the ends of her hair and kissed the crumbs off her mouth. "I'm glad you're safe. I'm glad Lulu's safe. How's your neck?"

"In need of pain relief. How's your knee?"

Reaching down and squeezing it, he said, "Just another war wound."

He left her in the kitchen and clipped his holster onto his belt. He felt the side pocket of his jacket, his fingers tracing the oblong shape of the thumb drive. Jed would have some explaining to do today and, with any luck, so would Tony Fuentes.

Ashlynn had been unusually quiet on the drive to the tow yard. Had they made a mistake sleeping together? How could a mistake feel so good? But the act had introduced a level of awkwardness between them that hadn't existed before.

Maybe once this case was over, they could date like normal people. He didn't even know what that looked like anymore. Other women he'd gone out with in the past had accused him of being cold and aloof.

He'd tried that with Ashlynn, but she'd poked through his reserve. He huffed out a breath as he pulled onto the freeway. He'd better get a grip. He couldn't be detached when he'd found Ashlynn in danger—and she always seemed to be in danger. The heightened stakes had them colliding together. She'd wanted him last night because he'd rescued her, and he couldn't deny it to himself that he'd wanted her for the same reason.

Coming to the rescue still gave him a charge, but only if he succeeded. If he were to fail…again, he'd wind up in a very dark place.

After showering and changing at home, he drove to the station. He parked and burst inside with purpose driving his steps. He'd call Jed Gordon first thing and ask him about the video. Then he'd circle back to the Wexler campaign and ask them what they knew about Escalante's dirty tricks. Christian had finally sent over the list of volunteers, and it was no surprise that Tiana wasn't among them.

As he jogged upstairs, he passed Detective Marino, who slapped him on the back. "Good deal when the journos do our work for us, isn't it? I'm glad I let you take lead."

Denver almost tripped on the next step. "What?"

Marino waved his hand without answering, and Denver continued to his desk in Homicide, his steps decidedly slower. Was Marino directing that comment to him?

He yanked out his chair and fished the thumb drive out of his pocket. As he booted up his laptop,

Captain Fields poked her head into the room. "Holt, my office."

With his mouth dry, he glanced around the room, but nobody met his eyes. He was being paranoid. He was lead detective on the Tiana Fuller case. Of course, the captain wanted to talk to him.

He tossed the drive in the air and caught it, clenching his hand around it. He had something to show her.

Captain Fields was already behind her desk when he approached the door. "Captain?"

"Have a seat, Holt."

He kicked out the chair in front of her desk and sat back. He didn't want to put his anxiety on display. He waited while she tapped her keyboard.

When he heard Jed Gordon's voice talking to Tiana Fuller, the blood drained from his face and his hands gripped the arms of the chair like claws.

Captain Fields spun her laptop around to face him, but he didn't need to look at the video. "How is it that a blogger is getting more information about the Tiana Fuller case than you are, Holt?"

He relaxed his clenched jaw and tipped his closed fist over, dropping the thumb drive on the blotter in front of her. "I have the same thing. That's Jed Gordon, Councilwoman Escalante's campaign manager, and he's talking to Tiana Fuller."

Her gaze flicked to the thumb drive. "I know that already and so does half of LA. My question to you is, why did half the city know this before I did?"

He lifted a stiff shoulder. "I guess my source delivered this video to me and...*LA Confidential*."

"You say *LA Confidential* as if that's a person. Your source didn't deliver it to *LA Confidential*. He or she delivered it to Ashlynn Hughes—the enemy."

His eyebrows jumped. "Enemy. That's kinda strong. I—I mean, she's not her brother. Her brother was murdered, for God's sake."

Hadn't Ashlynn just become the enemy to him? A person who'd used him, slept with him, to pull a fast one. The captain was right.

"Don't get me wrong." Captain Fields ended the video. "What The Player did to Sean Hughes was despicable. Nobody in this department would say otherwise, but when you play with fire, you can expect to get burned."

He rubbed his knuckles along his jaw, feeling the singe. "I don't think Ashlynn is as bad as her brother."

She just might be worse.

"Nevertheless, I don't like being blindsided, Holt."

"I'm sorry, Captain, but I can't control my sources. If they want to communicate with the press, they have a right to do that." He swept up the thumb drive and rapped his knuckles on the desk. "I was about to get right on this. I interviewed Jed Gordon yesterday, and he told me at the time he'd never heard of or seen Tiana Fuller. He might just be my first suspect."

"Get to it, Holt. I just hope the blogger didn't spook Gordon."

"If he runs now, we have even more reason to suspect him."

"Don't make me regret taking a floater and making you lead detective on this, Holt." She waved her hand in dismissal.

"No, ma'am." So, he had Captain Field to thank for his position, not Marino.

As he walked back to his desk, he ground his back teeth. Why the hell was he defending Ashlynn to Captain Fields? She'd betrayed him.

Ashlynn hadn't been interested in her laptop this morning because she'd already written her blog and posted the video. When did she have time for that? Between kisses?

He slumped in his chair and brought up *LA Confidential* on his phone. He'd be damned if he'd let the other detectives catch him reading the blog on his laptop.

He didn't need to play the video, but he read the blog, his breath coming in short spurts as he cupped his hand over his cell. Damn, Ashlynn was a good writer.

The post had already garnered hundreds of comments. He'd cull through them for anything useful. What had Marino said... *journos do our work for us*? That might be good enough for Marino, but Denver wasn't about to let it happen on his watch.

He pulled Jed Gordon's card from the file on his desk, flicked the corner and then tucked it into his breast pocket. If Jed had any intention of running,

Denver didn't want to give him a head start by calling him first.

Grabbing the keys to his department vehicle, he called out to nobody in particular. "Heading out for an interview."

Billy yelled back at him. "Get there before the blogger."

Denver held up his middle finger as he strode out the door, a chorus of laughter erupting behind him.

Wait until they found out he'd slept with that blogger last night. That wouldn't come from him, but who knows what Ashlynn had planned in her quest for blog world dominance.

When he got to his car, he shrugged off his jacket, feeling warm under the collar already. He smoothed it onto the front seat and took off for the Escalante campaign headquarters. He didn't expect to find Ashlynn there. She'd been made.

He'd better find Jed there.

This time when he burst through the door, heads swiveled and eyes darted. Before he had a chance to open his mouth, demanding to see Jed Gordon, the man himself glided out of his office, hand outstretched.

"Detective, I expected to see you this morning. Please join me for coffee down the street."

Denver gripped the other man's hand and searched his drawn face, the eyes pleading for…something. Was there fear in that look?

Nodding, Denver said, "Just so happened, I missed my morning coffee."

Jed's shoulders sagged in relief before his lips stretched into a smile. "Excellent. We can walk."

Jed barked a few orders to the staff on the way out, and heaved a long breath when they hit the sidewalk.

Denver looked over at him. "Everyone see that video?"

Jed said through gritted teeth, "Yes, and I'd like to know where that…blogger got it."

"Why'd you lie, Gordon?"

Jed put his fingers to his forehead and closed his eyes. "Can we wait until I'm sitting down with some coffee in front of me?"

Denver sealed his lips and walked beside Jed in silence until they reached a coffeehouse on the corner. Jed ordered a complicated concoction while Denver opted for the daily brew—black. He picked up the tab to get on Jed's good side.

When they sat across from each other at a large table, Jed slurped from his coffee cup. A thin layer of foam coated his upper lip, but he didn't seem to notice. "I lied to you yesterday. I knew Tiana Fuller and asked her to spy on the Wexler campaign for us."

"Yeah, I know that now." Denver popped the lid on his cup and blew on the steaming liquid. "The question is why."

"Why do you think?"

"Let me ask the questions, Gordon." Denver drilled his finger into the table, and Jed jerked back, his coffee sloshing over the rim.

"I asked a young woman to put herself at risk by pulling a few dirty tricks on Wexler, and she was found in the trunk of a Wexler car in a grungy lake. That makes me, the campaign and Veronica look bad."

"Yeah, you should've seen how it made Tiana look."

Jed's eyes bulged. "I never meant that young woman to come to any harm—none of us did. These things happen between political opponents. A little mudslinging here, a little defamation there—it's all part of the political landscape. The voters believe what they want to believe anyway."

"Whose idea was it to enlist Tiana Fuller's help?"

"It was hers."

"Sure it was." Denver crumpled a paper napkin in his fist. "She came up with that plan all by herself."

"Not the actual plan, but the suggestion." Jed swirled his coffee, his tongue darting out to capture some foam from the surface of the liquid. "Why do you think I videoed it on my phone?"

Denver leaned forward, spreading his hands on the table. "Explain it to me like I'm real stupid."

"I—I figured if I had Tiana on record agreeing to the plan, if anything happened, I'd have proof that she was a willing participant."

"What did you expect to happen?"

"Not *murder*." Jed's hand trembled so much, he had to set his cup down. "What could Tiana have possibly found out about the Wexler campaign that led them to murder her?"

"'Them'?"

"Wexler's people." Jed waved his hands in the

air. "Isn't that obvious? The CREW found out Tiana was spying and took care of her...in one of their own cars."

Denver tented his fingers. "What *did* Tiana find out? Did she report anything to you?"

"She filed a few reports with me, but it was stupid, petty stuff. She discovered some of the Wexler volunteers were ripping down Escalante posters, creating fake social media accounts to bolster Wexler and criticize Escalante—that kind of thing. Do you think anything like that warrants murder?"

"Not one for politics, but I can't imagine it would. Was she working on something? Did she ever indicate to you that she'd discovered something big?" Denver's phone dinged in his pocket, signaling an incoming text, but he ignored it. He wasn't ready to hear Ashlynn's excuses or apologies.

"Never. Like I said before, all minor league stuff."

"Did Councilwoman Escalante know about Tiana's role in the campaign?"

"No!" Jed folded his hands around his cup, his face reddening. "She called me this morning and read me the riot act when she saw that video."

Denver traced a finger around the rim of his cup, his eyes downcast to the dark liquid he'd barely tasted. "Was she mad that you recruited Tiana to spy, or was she mad that you made the video and got caught?"

"Veronica is clean." Jed pounded his fist on the table and the little packets of sugar danced.

Denver held up his hands. "She's a politician. You just said this was common practice."

"Among the campaign workers."

"Oh, okay." Denver nodded slowly. "How did Tiana get all this information for you?"

Shrugging, Jed said, "I don't know. I didn't ask, and she didn't tell."

"What did you mean earlier when you said this spying was Tiana's idea?"

"Just that. She's the one who suggested it. Said she had some contacts in the CREW and she could use them to get some dirt on Wexler."

"That's not on the video." Denver drummed his fingers on the table. He still didn't get why Jed had lied to him about Tiana's role in the campaign if she'd just discovered minor infractions.

"I—I couldn't get my phone in place fast enough to record the beginning of our meeting, but trust me. Tiana came on as a volunteer, bumped into me at a lunch spot down the street and made her case. Of course, I jumped on it."

"How come none of the other volunteers know Tiana, or were they lying, too?"

"Lulu gave Tiana the tour." Jed took a sip of his coffee and choked on it.

Had he just realized who'd stolen the video from his computer?

Jed cleared his throat. "Lulu got her signed up, and then destroyed Tiana's paperwork on my command. If Tiana got caught Watergate-style, I didn't want it to come back and bite us."

"If that's all that had happened." Denver fished his phone from his pocket after the second insistent ping and glanced at the unknown number, and the beginning of a text with his name.

"Are we finished here?" Jed pointed to Denver's phone. "Looks like you're busy, and I have to get back to it. I'll tell you anything you want, Detective. I don't have anything to hide, and neither does Veronica."

"Good, because I plan to pay her a visit." Denver lifted his cup. "You can leave. I'll stay and finish my coffee."

He watched Jed exit the coffeehouse, already on his phone. Was Jed warning Veronica? He seemed to worship the woman. The two of them had probably been discussing Tiana at the fundraiser last night when Ashlynn had seen them by the pool.

He tapped the insistent text, and adrenaline pumped through his system. Tiana's friend, Tony Fuentes, had finally surfaced and wanted to meet with him. He called the number on the text, but it went straight to a generic voice mail.

Two minutes later, Tony texted him that he couldn't talk on the phone but would meet with him in Venice by the pier. Why did everyone want to meet in Venice all of a sudden?

They arranged a meet location, and Denver took his coffee to keep him company on the long trip to the west side of the city. He could stop by Escalante's place on the way back to the station.

When he slid behind the wheel, he reached for

his phone to text Ashlynn to tell her about Tony. He dropped it in the cup holder instead. Ashlynn Hughes could wait.

By the time he reached the Venice Pier, he had the AC blasting. They'd just come off a week of scattered showers, but the sun had been making a stronger appearance ever since and had hit peak Southern California spring beach day.

He parked in the lot next to the strand and left his jacket in the car. He stepped onto the asphalt, the sand crunching beneath his shoes. He couldn't do anything about his wingtips, but he could lose the tie.

He loosened his tie, pulled it over his head and undid the top buttons of his shirt. He dropped his tie on top of his jacket and locked up. He usually didn't leave anything on the seat of his car, especially in an area like this, but he figured the local beach transients wouldn't be interested in stealing his jacket and tie.

As he clumped through the dry sand, he rolled up his sleeves. Tony couldn't have picked a worse location, but Denver didn't want to spook the skittish boyfriend.

He spotted a figure beneath the pier and trudged over the beach toward him. As he drew closer, another person appeared next to the pilings, red hair streaming behind her in the breeze.

Denver's heart rattled his ribs. What the hell was Ashlynn doing here—at his meeting?

He picked up the pace and hit wet sand, veering to his right. "Tony Fuentes?"

The young man with a beard gathered his shoulder-length dark hair with one hand. "That's me. Detective Holt?"

Denver gripped Tony's hand and said, "Now that we've established who we are, can I ask why she's here?"

"Why do you think, Denver?" Ashlynn released her hair to put her hands on her hips, and the red locks caught fire from the sun as they whipped around her face. "This is my source."

Tony raised his hand. "Anthony Angel Fuentes, at your service."

Chapter Sixteen

Ashlynn sucked in her bottom lip. Denver looked ready to explode. She hadn't planned on contacting him today, hadn't even told him about this meeting with Angel, but when she'd seen Denver scuffing through the dry sand and realized Angel had called him, too, she wasn't going to run away. She wanted to hear what Angel had to say.

Denver closed his eyes for a second and wiped the back of his hand over his gleaming forehead. She felt for him. He must be burning up in that suit, or half a suit. He certainly *looked* hot.

"Why did you contact a blogger about Tiana's murder instead of the police, and I mean right from the beginning?"

Tony hunched his thin shoulders, his T-shirt billowing around his gaunt frame. "I was scared, dude. I wasn't sure you'd connect me to T, and I didn't want to expose myself. I don't wanna be next."

Denver held up his phone. "I'm recording this interview."

Not waiting for Tony's approval, Denver recorded

the date and time, along with Tony's name. Then he went straight for the jugular. "Do you know who killed Tiana?"

"I don't know who did it." Tony ran his fingers through his beard. "I—I only know how they disposed of her body."

Ashlynn asked, "How do you know that? How did you know about the car in the lake?"

Denver had turned his back to her, as if he could cut her out of his exchange with Tony. As if Tony hadn't contacted her, too. As if she wasn't a part of this investigation just as much as he was.

She pushed her way into their circle.

"I saw it happen." Tony ducked his head and his long hair curtained his face. When he looked up, he had tears in his eyes. "I knew T was meeting someone. I told her not to go. I warned her. She wouldn't listen to me."

"I know the feeling." Denver's jaw formed a hard line. "Who was she meeting? What did she find out about the Wexler campaign that led to her murder?"

"Dude, I don't know. She wouldn't tell me."

Ashlynn curled her toes into the wet sand. "How did you and Tiana know each other, school?"

"Yeah, we had a few poli-sci classes together." Tony wiped his face and sniffled. "I'm the one who got her to volunteer for the campaigns in the first place. It's my fault she's dead."

"Hold on a minute." Denver unbuttoned another button of his shirt. "Campaigns? How many campaigns did Tiana work for?"

Tony blinked. "Just the two."

"Two? What two? You lost me."

Denver finally glanced at her, a question in his eyes, but she quickly lifted and dropped her shoulders. Tony hadn't told her a thing.

"The Escalante and Wexler campaigns. She worked for both of them."

Denver's wide eyes and open mouth reflected her own feelings, and she took advantage of his momentary loss for words.

"Tiana wasn't very dedicated to either candidate, was she? Or was she just trying to get as much experience as possible?"

"Oh, no. She was dedicated to re-electing Mayor Wexler. We both were—are."

Denver had recovered and got in the question hovering on her own lips. "If she was pro Wexler, why was she working for the Escalante campaign and in that particular capacity?"

"Dude, I thought you knew." Tony turned his head and spit into the sand. "She was working for the Escalante campaign as a mole. She was team CREW all the way."

Folding his arms, Denver said, "Dude, I didn't know that. How was I supposed to know that with you playing hide-and-seek and slipping tips to a *blogger* instead of the police?"

Ashlynn's blood simmered as Tony's eyes darted between her and Denver. "I figured you already talked to the CREW."

"I did talk to them—Amalia Fernandez and Christian Bushnell, to be precise. Both denied knowledge of Tiana Fuller."

"Dude, that sucks." Shaking his head, Tony covered his face. "I don't know why they're playing that game. Christian knows Tiana. He's the one T told about her plan to infiltrate Escalante's campaign."

Denver ran a hand through his hair. "Was that all Tiana's plan or Christian's?"

"That was all T, man." Tony grinned through his beard. "That girl was fearless. She suggested it to Christian and he gave his stamp of approval, but even if he hadn't, she would've done it, anyway. Then she joined the Escalante campaign and suggested to *them* that she spy on Wexler."

"How do you know she wasn't really working for Escalante and spying on Wexler?" Ashlynn glanced at Denver. "She was found in a Wexler car, not an Escalante car."

"I thought about that, but no way. She was all-in for Wexler. She was especially in favor of his slow-growth policies for the city. You see what Escalante and her husband are planning for downtown?"

"Slow down." Denver drew a line in the sand with the toe of his shoe. "That could've been her plan, but maybe she actually discovered some dirt about Wexler—dirty enough to result in murder."

"I can't believe that." Tony had the ring of the true believer in his voice.

"Let's go back to the car in the lake." Denver wiped the face of his phone on his pant leg. "How did you manage to witness that?"

"T had shared her phone's location with me weeks before her murder. Maybe she forgot, because I did. But when she didn't call me after her meeting, I freaked. Then I remembered she'd shared her location, and I brought it up on my phone. I couldn't figure out why she was heading out toward Angeles Crest, but I had a bad feeling. I followed the phone, and it took me to Lake Kawayu. The phone stopped working at that point, but I got there just in time to see two guys pushing a car into the lake."

Ashlynn covered her mouth. "Why didn't you call 9-1-1? Tiana could've still been alive."

"She wasn't!" Tony grabbed his hair at the roots, looking like a wild man. He turned wide eyes on Denver. "Tell me she wasn't. Tell me she didn't drown in that trunk while I watched from my safe distance."

Denver's voice had a rough edge when he answered the feverish question. "She wasn't. They shot her before they put her in the trunk. The coroner didn't find any water in her lungs. Did you get a good look at the two men?"

"No, but I swear they heard me. They definitely heard my car. I think they might be after me." Tony sank to his knees in the wet sand and sobbed. "I'm such a coward. Maybe I could've saved her."

Denver dropped his hand to the young man's shoulder. "I don't think so, Tony. You're doing the right thing now. We're going to find out who did this, and you're going to do the right thing by T and testify, right?"

"I will, I will." Tony dragged a hand across his runny nose. "Dude, I gotta go now. My ride's coming."

Denver ended the recording on his phone. "I can reach you at the number you used to text me?"

"Yeah, it's a burner, but I'm keeping it." Tony staggered to his feet. "Don't put this in *LA Confidential*. The CREW will know it's me, and I just can't right now."

"I'll figure out something. You're helping Tiana now, Tony." She squeezed his arm. "Just keep cooperating with Detective Holt."

That earned her a quick glance from Denver.

"For sure." Tony wiped his face on his T-shirt and jogged down the beach on the packed sand.

Ashlynn pulled her sweater around her as the breeze from the ocean picked up. "Wow, this is a tangled web. Tiana was playing with fire any way you look at it—a double agent."

"Maybe, but she didn't get murdered for being a mole. She discovered something more serious than dirty tricks that someone wanted to keep quiet."

Ashlynn licked her lips, tasting the salt from the air. "I'm sorry I didn't tell you about posting that video on the blog. I had to do it, and I knew you'd object."

Denver shoved his hands in his pockets and stared at the ocean, roiling and spitting just a few feet in front of them, the spray clinging to his dark hair, making it curl at the ends.

"I have to hand it to you. You pulled a fast one,

seducing me, getting me into bed so that you could sneak back and copy the video to your laptop."

Her jaw dropped. "Th-that's not... I didn't..."

"Save it for your readers. It might even make a good post for the almighty blog—how you tricked an LAPD wannabe homicide detective into leaving important evidence in your possession."

Tears stung her eyes as she reached out for him. "That's not why I slept with you. Making love with you last night was the first real joy I've felt since my brother died. The first time I've felt real and whole."

"Good for you."

As she watched him trudge through the sand back to the strand through blurred vision, one tear fell over the rim of her eye and ran down her cheek.

Looked like her brother had won again.

Chapter Seventeen

Denver's lead foot pressed against the accelerator in his zeal to get away from the beach and Ashlynn as quickly as possible—before he changed his mind about her.

Funny thing was, he'd felt the same way about last night—a connection with her, something solid and real after dozens of dates where he'd been afraid to scratch beneath any surface level.

He muttered to himself. "That's what she wanted you to feel."

He cruised down the freeway to the house of Veronica Escalante and her husband Kent Meadows. Meadows was a fat cat who had supported his younger wife's political aspirations. Escalante had recused herself from a few city council votes that had involved city planning where her husband could directly benefit. Still seemed shady to him.

He pulled up to the same drive he'd sat across from last night, but the valet attendants and lights were gone. In their place, gardeners worked the landscaping in the front of the house, the noise from their leaf blowers reverberating in the air.

When Denver got out of his vehicle, he waved and the gardener wielding the blower cut the motor. Denver called out, "Thanks."

He ascended the steps to the front door and pressed the doorbell, stepping back in case some-one wanted to get a look at him from the peephole or the cameras in the corner.

A female voice came over a speaker. "Who is it, please?"

Denver unclipped the badge from his belt and held it up. "Detective Holt, LAPD, ma'am. I need to talk to Councilwoman Escalante."

"Just a minute, please."

At least she was polite as she left him out on the porch in the heat. A minute later, the door opened and a woman, her hair in a tight bun, with a tighter smile, stood before him. "Come in, Detective. Would you like something to drink? Iced tea? Coffee? Water?"

"Nothing, thanks."

She bowed her head. "This way, please."

He followed her, the heels of his shoes clicking on the tile floor behind her crepe soles. She pushed open another door off the great room, all signs of the party vanished.

She took one step into the room, a library or of-fice, and said, "This is Detective Holt, Kent."

"Thanks, Mom." A fit-for-his-age man stood be-hind the desk, smoothing a hand along the side of his silver hair. He looked about the same age as *Mom*. "Detective, have a seat. I'm Kent Meadows."

Denver strode into the room and leaned across the desk to shake Meadows's hand; the older man's grip firm and practiced.

"Your wife isn't home?"

Meadows smiled, his blue eyes twinkling. "Ah, the demands of a campaign. I didn't want you to waste your time, Detective. Who knows? Veronica might show up before we're finished here."

Denver jerked his thumb over his shoulder. "Mom?"

"Rita is my mother-in-law."

"She works for you?"

Meadows waved his hands, his fingers tapering to a polished manicure. "Unofficial hostess. She lives in the appropriately named mother-in-law quarters in the back of the property—her own house—that she shares with Lulu, Veronica's sister. What can we help you with, Detective? I'm sure you're here about that unfortunate incident with that girl in the lake."

"Incident? It was a homicide, and your wife's campaign manager is on video with that girl in the lake, asking her to spy on Wexler's campaign."

"Of course, of course." Meadows folded his hands on his desk. "Tragic. I assume you've talked to Jed Gordon."

"I spoke with him. He couldn't deny the video, but said Veronica had nothing to do with the request."

The nostrils of Meadows's patrician nose flared. "Jed would say anything to protect Veronica."

Denver raised his eyebrows. "You don't believe him? Do you think your wife knew about Tiana Fuller?"

"Oh, I believe him. My wife doesn't concern herself too much with the volunteers or the nuts and bolts of the campaign. I take care of the financing and Jed takes care of the details, and Veronica does what she does best—connects with the people."

"I was hoping to talk to Veronica to find out if Jed told her anything about Tiana or what she may have discovered about the Wexler campaign."

Meadows eased back in his chair and flicked the drapes behind him, revealing a view of the meticulously tended garden in front of the house. "You're in luck, Detective Holt. My wife just pulled up to the house, but she looks busy. She's on her cell phone and she's not even out of the car yet."

"I won't take up too much of her time." Denver pushed back from the desk to get a view of Veronica Escalante stepping from a Porsche, teetering on a pair of stiletto heels, her phone to her ear, a bag slung over her shoulder.

Denver's gaze shifted from the window to a credenza behind Meadows, boasting several photos of construction sites. He pointed to one. "That's the Meadows Plaza downtown, right?"

Meadows's eyes flicked like a lizard's in his tanned face. "I hope it will be. Construction has stalled for the moment, but it should resume shortly."

"Shortly, as in when your wife gets elected mayor of LA?"

Meadows's lips stretched into a smile, but this time there was no twinkling of the eyes. "That's not how it operates, Detective."

"Are you waiting to see me?" Councilwoman Escalante's voice sounded different from her commercials and speeches. She'd lost the Spanish accent she put on for public appearances.

As Denver turned toward her, Meadows said, "This is Detective Holt, Veronica. Of course, he has some questions about that idiot Gordon and the video of him and that murdered girl. Why did he try to hide it in the first place?"

"You know Jed, my love." Veronica strode forward, her heels sinking into the thick carpet. She shook Denver's hand with a feminine hold, which she ended quickly.

She skirted him and placed a kiss on her husband's forehead. "Thank you for filling in for me, *mi amor*."

Meadows hopped up from his chair, his wife in those heels besting him by about three inches. "You two use my office. I've had a long day. I'm going to rustle up a drink before dinner. I'll be out at the pool, *mi vida*."

The Meadows kissed again, and Denver felt in danger of choking on saccharine sweetness if he stayed in their presence much longer. Was this lovey-dovey stuff for his benefit? He didn't even vote.

Meadows touched his fingers to his forehead as he left the room. "Nice meeting you, Detective. Good to see my donations to the Police Protective League not going to waste."

Whatever that meant.

Veronica sat in a leather love seat against the wall, crossing her shapely legs. "Only my husband sits behind his desk, Detective Holt. Have a seat and let me know how I can help. I feel terrible that Tiana worked for our campaign and that Jed knew it and wasn't forthcoming when you first questioned him. I've already talked to Jed about that, but surely any dirty tricks Tiana played on the Wexler campaign didn't result in her murder. That's just crazy to think that. Nobody gets murdered over tearing down flyers."

Typical politician. He'd have to talk fast to get a word in. "Did you ever meet or talk to Tiana?"

"No, I usually don't interact with the volunteers except to give pep talks or maybe buy pizzas." She flashed a fake smile. "They're invited to certain events, like our fundraiser last night."

"Have you seen Tiana's picture? Did you recognize her from any of those occasions?"

She squinted her dark eyes. "I did see her picture— pretty girl—but I had never seen her before, and if Jed was using her for undercover work, he probably wouldn't have invited her to any of the events."

"Did Jed tell you what Tiana had discovered about Wexler?"

"I told you, Detective. I didn't know anything about Tiana until after the video, and Jed told me what I'm sure he told you—petty tricks. We don't know anything about Wexler, except that he's not for LA at this time, and we're going to turn things around, including with the LAPD. Mayor Wexler and Chief Sterling are too cozy. The LAPD needs more oversight." She winked. "Although I'm sure you don't."

Denver held out one hand. "I'm not here to discuss LAPD policies, Councilwoman. I suppose Jed had no inkling that Tiana was actually a mole."

"What?" Veronica's confidence wavered with her voice. "What are you talking about?"

"According to one of my sources, Tiana didn't support you at all. She was all for Wexler and was playing Jed to get into your campaign."

Veronica's face paled. "That little...bi...sneak. She really wanted to get down and dirty, didn't she? If you're suggesting she might've discovered anything about our campaign, I can shut down that line of thinking right now. We play by the rules."

"Of course." Denver rose, leveling a finger at the photo of the Meadows Plaza construction site. "Too bad that project is stalled. Would be nice for downtown."

Veronica flicked a strand of dark hair over her shoulder as she rose from the love seat. "I'll let you know if I learn anything else about Tiana. Does Jed know she was a mole?"

"Not yet, but I'm sure you'll tell him. I'll see myself out." As Denver transitioned from the office to the great room, he let out a breath.

He sure hoped Escalante came across better with her constituents. She put him on edge.

The gardeners were planting a new bed of flowers under the direction of Veronica's mother as he maneuvered down the walkway. When he reached the gate, Mrs. Escalante touched the sleeve of his jacket.

He jerked his head around and she put her finger to her lips. "You're here about that murdered girl?"

"I am. Do you know something about her, Mrs. Escalante?"

She glanced over her shoulder at the house. "Just that she was here several times, *muchos tiempos*."

Chapter Eighteen

Ashlynn glanced between her phone and the door of the high-rise office building, as she sipped an iced tea on the patio of the office complex. The tall buildings created a wind tunnel and bits of debris swirled in mini tornadoes. She pushed her hair out of her face and replied to Lulu's text.

Veronica's sister had contacted her earlier to let her know she was okay and to inquire about her well-being. Once they'd assured each other that they were unharmed, Lulu had pressed her for information about her friend.

Ashlynn had Lulu half convinced already that he was just a friend looking out for them. He hadn't even known why they were meeting.

She had asked Lulu if she'd been followed to the dog park and if she'd recognized the man who had accosted them, and now she sat tapping her toe, waiting for a reply.

Glancing up as the office door swung open, she stuffed her phone in her purse. Lulu's response would have to wait.

She jumped to her feet, her ponytail swinging be-hind her, and caught up with the fresh-faced young man hurrying from the office building, a stack of folders beneath one arm.

"Christian?"

He swung around, almost dropping the files. "Y-yes. Do I know you?"

"Not yet." Ashlynn gave an encouraging smile. Christian needed kid-glove handling, which was probably why Denver hadn't gotten anything out of him. Had he tried again after their meeting with Tony? He wouldn't have had time—or at least Chris-tian wouldn't look so carefree if he'd just come from a meeting with Detective Holt.

Christian tipped his head, a shy smile curling one corner of his mouth. "I'm sorry?"

She hated to disrupt the happy vibe here, but someone had to do it. Taking a few steps in his direc-tion, she thrust out her hand. "I'm Ashlynn Hughes from *LA Confidential*."

You would've thought she'd told him she was from the IRS with an audit request the way the color drained from his face and then all came rush-ing back, staining his cheeks in a crimson tide.

"I—I don't have anything to say to you. We al-ready talked to that detective, gave him our volun-teer list. That's all." He pressed his lips together, as if willing himself to be quiet.

"You talked to Detective Holt today?"

"Today?" He gulped, his Adam's apple bobbing

in the slim column of his throat. "A few days ago. Is he coming back?"

"He just might." Ashlynn shifted her gaze to the side without turning her head, indicating they could expect him at any time. "But you can talk to me instead…and it's all confidential. I won't report your name. You don't have to testify to anything. Just between us."

"What do you want from me?" He hugged the folders to his chest, a poor substitute for armor. "I don't know anything about Tiana Fuller."

"I know that's not true, and Detective Holt's gonna know soon enough." She didn't have to terrify him any more by letting him know Denver already knew.

She took a step back toward the table and her iced tea. "Let's sit down a minute. I'm not going to record you or report your name. I just want to verify some information for my blog. It doesn't have to be about you, or even the Wexler campaign."

He followed her to the table, his gait stiff, and sat across from her, folding his thin frame in half. "What do you know? Or what do you think you know?"

She wrapped her ponytail around her hand and sucked in her bottom lip. "I know that Tiana did work for the CREW, that she was dedicated to re-electing Mayor Wexler—just like I am. I know that she offered to infiltrate the Escalante campaign as a spy, and then she pretended to fulfill the same role there as she actually had with the CREW. How am I doing so far?"

Christian's head dropped once. "That's what she was doing, but I didn't tell her to do it. Nobody did. That was just Tiana. She wanted to do it, thought it would be fun."

"Okay, okay." She folded her hands in front of her. "Tiana was an adult. I'm sure she made her own decisions. But what happened? What did she discover?"

"It wasn't about us." Christian crossed his hands over his chest. "I swear. She didn't find anything on Mayor Wexler. She wasn't even looking. She was digging into Escalante, not the mayor. She had no access to anything at our campaign headquarters. She never even came in."

"You think she found out something about Escalante?" She tapped her fingernails against her plastic cup.

"She must have, but she didn't tell me." He snapped his fingers. "She might've told one of the other volunteers—Tony. They were tight."

Been there, done that.

"How did she wind up in the trunk of one of your cars?"

"I can't tell you. I couldn't tell the cops, either. Honestly, nobody keeps tabs on those cars. I've known volunteers to take them out to pick up lunch and bring them back four days later, nobody the wiser. Tiana herself used the cars sometimes."

"She never gave you any hint about what she was working on? What she might've found?"

"Nothing, but she seemed…"

"What?" Ashlynn hunkered forward. "Go on."

"Secretly satisfied?" He rubbed his clean-shaved chin, which looked as if it had never experienced razor burn. "You might think she'd have been worried with all the subterfuge, but she seemed pleased about something. That's how I'd describe it. That's why I was so shocked when I found out she'd been murdered. She was happy, not scared."

"Maybe she didn't know enough to be scared, but she should've been." Ashlynn rattled the ice in her cup. "How come you didn't tell Detective Holt any of this?"

"First of all, he interviewed me with my boss. If I had said one word, I would've been fired. This is a paid gig for me. I got the feeling Detective Holt wanted to get me on my own. He's been leaving me messages, and I've been avoiding them."

"This is a woman's life here, Christian. It's not fun and political games."

"You don't think politics are life and death? Neither did Tiana, and look what happened to her." He straightened the files on the table. "Amalia doesn't want it known that one of our volunteers was murdered. It's bad enough that Tiana was found in one of our cars. Looks like the Escalante campaign didn't want to claim her, either."

"Poor Tiana. Both campaigns were eager to use her, and then disowned her when she needed them."

After she assured Christian she wouldn't use his name in her blog, he escaped to where he was headed when she'd waylaid him.

She checked her phone for Lulu's response to her

most recent text, but she hadn't answered the all-important question of whether or not she'd been fol-lowed last night. She had assured Ashlynn that she had left town and was keeping a low profile, espe-cially as Jed had accused her of stealing and then leaking the video.

She sucked down the rest of her tea and took a big breath. Before running to her blog to release this latest piece of information, she had some amends to make first.

She couldn't believe Denver thought she'd se-duced him just to post that video before he could question Jed. It looked bad, but she'd wanted that man from the get-go, and it had nothing to do with *LA Confidential*—for once.

She called Denver and held her breath as his phone rang. Would he brush her off?

He picked up after the third ring. "Yeah."

"I'm going to apologize without saying sorry."

He huffed out a long breath. "You like playing games, Ashlynn. I don't."

"Yeah, like dissing me at lunch the other day after we'd been getting along great was not some kind of maneuver?"

"I think I made up for that, or I thought I did. Didn't realize I was getting handled."

"Now I'm going to make it up to you. I have some information from Christian Bushnell, and I'm coming to you first instead of splashing it all over my blog."

He caught his breath. "I have some information, too."

She smacked her palm on the table for her own benefit. "Then let's get together and return to our original purpose."

"Dinner tonight?"

Her heart fluttered in her chest. "I'd love to have dinner with you and compare notes."

"Marina, The Warehouse, seven o'clock."

He ended the call before she even had a chance to respond. There was only one response to give. Whether Denver Holt believed her not, she might be ready to put something or someone ahead of the blog.

For once, she was more excited to see Denver than to hear the information he had about the case. Would he believe her?

DENVER TOOK A sip of beer through the thick head on the top. He had to be out of his mind. He should be sharing this information with Marino, not Ashlynn, even though she had worked harder on this case than Marino had. Could he trust that she wouldn't run off to post it for her followers?

She wouldn't if he explained to her how it could compromise the case. The video of Jed and Tiana hadn't done that. He'd had no intention of tiptoeing around Jed Gordon, but this piece of knowledge demanded a certain level of secrecy.

He spied Ashlynn on the edge of the bar, surveying the dining tables. When their eyes met, he felt an electric shock.

She raised her hand and strode toward him with those long legs, her hair bright against a black top.

Her black jeans and boots just made her look like one long, lean line of sexy.

She slid into the booth, across from him, and lifted the purse slung across her body over her head. She nodded at the big window overlooking slips of bobbing boats. "This is…touristy."

"It's kind of my local. I can walk here." He tapped the side of his glass. "Sorry I started without you. It's been a helluva day."

"Tell me about it. I can't believe Tony watched while two men stuffed his friend's body in the trunk of car, and then pushed that car into a lake, and didn't do one thing about it." She glanced up as the waitress approached. "Glass of chardonnay, house is fine."

"I could see where he was coming from. Even if he called the police at that point, nothing could've been done for Tiana." He sat back and folded his arms. "At least he contacted you."

She folded the corner of the napkin the waitress had tossed in front of her. "I saw Christian Bushnell today."

"Let me guess." He caught a bead of moisture from the outside of his glass with the tip of his finger. "You got more out of him than I did."

"I caught him alone, without his boss hovering. I think you would've gotten to him eventually. He's not a very good liar, and I don't think he likes lying."

"He's in the wrong business. What did he tell you?"

"Not too much. He verified Tony's story about Tiana working for the CREW. Just like Jed, Christian maintained that the spying angle was Tiana's idea."

"Hmm." He scratched his chin and gulped down some beer as the waitress delivered Ashlynn's wine.

She wrapped a finger around the stem. "Hmm, what?"

"You told me over the phone that you had some news for me. That's hardly news. We already got that from Tony."

She blinked and took a careful sip of her wine. "There's more. He said Tiana wasn't scared or worried, that she seemed pleased about something. He also said anyone could've taken one of the vehicles. Tiana herself could've taken one of the cars."

"Okay, but he didn't know what she'd discovered over there?"

"He didn't have a clue. Sounds like she was keeping things to herself. Honestly?" She pinged her glass and the golden liquid inside shimmered. "I just wanted to see you. To apologize for how my actions appeared to you. Sure, I didn't want you nixing my post with the video, but I swear I did not use sex to get one over on you. I would've found a way to copy that video to my laptop, whether you spent the night with me or not."

"You're not apologizing for posting the video on your blog?"

Her eyebrows jumped. "Absolutely not. It drove people to the blog, and it didn't hurt your case. You know it didn't, Denver."

"It got me in some hot water with my captain, it gave Jed a heads-up. He could've bolted."

"Leaving Veronica? Never."

"There are some tips that aren't meant for public consumption. You know that, right?"

"I never revealed that Tiana was found in a CREW car, did I?"

"Ready to order?" Their waitress had finally taken the plunge after hovering every time she passed their table.

Ashlynn's gaze flicked over the menu. "I'll have the crab cakes appetizer and a side salad."

"Sea bass for me, please."

After the waitress clarified a few more details about their order and left, Denver hunched forward. "If I tell you something now, you have to promise to keep it out of *LA Confidential*. This is too important, Ashlynn. More important than the blog."

"I understand." She pressed a hand to her chest. "I promise, Denver."

"It has to do with something you mentioned earlier, on the night of the fundraiser. That's why I want to run it by you."

"The argument between Veronica and Jed?"

"No, an offhand comment by the volunteers. They said Kent Meadows was a manther."

Her giggle ended in a choke when she realized he was serious. "Kent Meadows? What do his personal preferences have to do with anything?"

"I went out to the house to talk to Veronica about that video and to find out what she knew about Tiana's role in the campaign. She denied knowing of Tiana's existence."

"She's lying. She and Jed were arguing about

something that night, but what does this have to do with her husband?"

"I'm getting there. Did you know Veronica's mother lives with them?"

Ashlynn nodded. "She lives in a guest cottage in the back, with Lulu."

"Mrs. Escalante was there today and, when I was leaving, she pulled me aside and told me that Tiana had been to the house."

"Well, that sort of proves Veronica was lying, doesn't it?"

"Maybe not." Denver drummed his fingers on the table. "Mrs. Escalante told me Tiana was there to see Kent."

Chapter Nineteen

Ashlynn covered her mouth with her hand. "Kent? Tiana was there to see Kent?"

"That's what Mrs. Escalante told me. She said Tiana had been to the house several times, and I just assumed she meant to see her daughter. But she corrected me, and said only Kent was home when Tiana was there."

"Unless Mrs. Escalante was lying to protect her daughter." Ashlynn toyed with her napkin. Denver was right. This information didn't belong in the blog...not yet.

"I thought about that, but then why tell me anything at all? I wasn't questioning Mrs. Escalante. I was on my way out the front gate when she grabbed me. She didn't have to say a word."

"What does it mean? I don't think Kent is even that involved with the campaign. He's strictly the money guy."

"Strictly the money guy and the guy who hits on young women. What better source of young, eager women than your wife's election campaign?" He moved his beer to the side to make room for the plates in their waitress's hands.

"Anything else? Refill on the drinks?"

They both declined the second drink, and Ashlynn shook out her napkin. "You think Kent and Tiana were hooking up?"

She wrinkled her nose as she asked the question, and he didn't think it had to do with the savory smells coming from their food.

"Hooking up might be too strong. Maybe they were having some kind of flirtation." He dragged a fork through his garlic-mashed potatoes. "You picked up on that vibe in the video with Jed, right?"

She waved her fork at him. "Hold on. You're not blaming the victim here, are you? Whatever Tiana did or whatever methods she may have used to get information, none of that deserves a death sentence."

A muscle twitched in his jaw. "I did not say that, and I'm not implying it at all, but it might explain what she was doing with Kent Meadows. She saw his weakness and went in for the kill. We already know she was willing to take risks for the thrill of the hunt."

"She cozies up to Kent, gets invited to the house while the candidate is campaigning, and discovers… what?"

"We already established that Kent wasn't interested in the nuts and bolts of the election, but it doesn't mean Tiana couldn't discover things in that house that could benefit Wexler—maybe something so big, Kent had to keep her quiet."

Ashlynn scooted up to the edge of the booth. "And what's so big to Kent right now? We've been thinking politics all this time, but maybe Tiana found out about something else."

"Meadows Plaza. The project is currently on hold. Why?"

"I can write a post tomorrow about Meadows Plaza, see what my readers know about it."

"We don't want to tip off Meadows. So far, he believes we think he's Veronica Escalante's Mr. Moneybags, nothing more. If you and your readers go snooping around Kent Meadows and Meadows Plaza, we're giving him a heads-up." He pointed his fork at her. "You're not the only one with sources. I know a guy in Building and Planning. I'm sure he can give me the lowdown on Meadows Plaza."

Ashlynn poked at her salad, a shiver of excitement giving her goose bumps. "I think we're really on to something, Denver. Thank you for sharing that with me."

"The other night—" he dragged a napkin across his mouth "—it felt like you used me to post that video on your blog. I don't like being used, and it made me look like a fool in front of my captain."

"I know." She gripped the edge of the table. "I didn't think how it would look for you, being in the dark. At that point, it was more important for me to get that blog out."

"Why is it such a big deal for you to prove yourself with that blog? It's kind of toxic. I think you need to strike out on your own." He threw back the rest of his beer. "And that's as far as I'll go."

"I know you're right. My parents were perfectionists in everything they did when Sean and I were growing up—still are. It's just that Sean seemed to do everything right, and I was the eternal screw-up. So, I started controlling the one thing that was all mine—eating. I became anorexic and my supermodel mom didn't even realize it until I fainted. Even after family therapy, my mom didn't acknowledge her role in my eating disorder—not that I'm blaming her." She held up her hand. "That was all me, and I was no angel."

Denver reached for her hand and smoothed his thumb across the inside of her wrist. "Having an eating disorder doesn't make you a bad person."

"How about outing your own brother?"

He cocked his head. "What do you mean?"

"I found out Sean was gay. I knew he wanted to tell my parents in his own way and time, and I should've allowed him that space, but I thought I could finally get one over on him. I figured my parents would be upset when they found out their only son was gay, so I blabbed it to them. I felt terrible when Sean found out what I'd done. And the funny thing is? My parents didn't care at all, which is how it should be, and I'm glad they reacted the way they did. The whole thing blew up in my face. I was the bad guy."

"Not cool, but how old were you?"

"A teenager—no excuse. I just wanted to be the chosen one for a change."

"How did Sean react to all of this? From what I've heard about him, he was no angel, either. I mean he called out my mom as a murderer based on some life insurance and an extramarital affair."

Ashlynn had read that whole blog series and could see where Sean was coming from, but she'd never admit that to Denver. "You're right. Sean had his issues. He knew he was the favored one. He didn't exactly lord it over me, but he reveled in it. We made our peace before he died. I'm thankful for that."

"Now this blog is hanging over your head as a way to prove yourself worthy in your parents' eyes and maybe to make up for what you did to Sean. But just like the food was controlling you, not the other way around, this blog is controlling you."

"Your father's murder doesn't control you to an extent?"

"It does, but it also dovetails with what I want to do with my life—solve homicides. I'm not sure the blog is what you want to do with your life."

"I'm not sure about that. I'm really pumped about the direction we're going with this case. It feels good." She sawed into her crab cake and held it up. "And I no longer have an eating disorder, in case you haven't noticed."

"I'm glad." He pointed to his plate. "Maybe you can help me with some of this."

"Ugh, you're not going to start watching what I

eat, are you? Whenever I tell people I had anorexia, they start counting my calories for me."

"I'm sure you can handle your own food intake. It's your obsession with *LA Confidential* that worries me."

THE NEXT MORNING, Denver updated both Marino and Captain Fields, letting them know he was going to look into Kent Meadows, as he'd gotten a tip that the councilwoman's husband may have known Tiana. Marino was happy he didn't have to do anything today except talk to some of Tiana's school friends in Long Beach, and Captain Fields was glad Denver had seemingly wrested control of the investigation from the blogger.

He didn't tell the captain about dinner last night.

Both he and Ashlynn had made the decision to sleep in their own beds. His ego needed some time to recover, and Ashlynn wanted a chance to prove herself to him.

Her blog today had focused on Tiana, paying tribute to a bright and energetic young woman lost too soon. She hit all the right notes and had managed to draw even more people into the story of "The Girl in the Lake."

Maybe he was wrong and this blog was her true calling. He just hated seeing her try so hard for validation from her parents that would most likely never come.

As soon as he sank into his chair and reached for the mouse, his contact at the Building and Planning office called him. He snatched up his phone. "Ebert, what do you have for me?"

Greg Ebert whistled across the line. "That Meadows Plaza project is in big trouble. Kent Meadows is never going to get that done. The dude owes money, he's being sued, we just rejected his most recent set of diagrams. He's going to lose a bundle."

"That's common knowledge, though, right? Or it could be if someone wanted to investigate the project."

"Sure, what are you getting at?"

"Secrets."

"I can tell you this, Holt. If that wife of his gets elected mayor, she could make a lot of his problems go away. It would have to be done on the sly, but this type of quid pro quo happens all the time."

"Okay, thanks, Ebert. I appreciate it."

Seemed like he needed to have a talk with Kent again—and this time he planned to get personal. He placed a call to Meadows and left a voice mail.

He spent the rest of the afternoon reviewing the ballistics report for the bullet that killed Tiana. He'd also gotten forensics for the car—all prints wiped clean, most evidence washed out in the lake—but the forensics team had discovered a few hairs in the trunk that didn't belong to Tiana and a few fibers.

Nobody had any idea where Tiana had been murdered, including Tony, and with the pithy evidence from the car, Denver needed something big. He needed a confession from Kent Meadows.

When his phone rang, his heart pounded when he saw Ashlynn's name. They hadn't touched base all day, and he still couldn't stop worrying about her although she'd abandoned her undercover gig at the Escalante campaign headquarters.

He picked up and said, "Is this the hot blogger who's breaking the case of the girl in lake?"

She laughed with a nervous edge. "You read the blog today, right?"

"It was good, and I appreciate your discretion. I know it wasn't easy, knowing what you do about Meadows."

"I just want you to know I'm all about solving this crime. I won't do anything to jeopardize that."

"I can see that, so I think I can tell you that Meadows is in trouble over that project."

She huffed out a breath. "That's apparent, though, isn't it? That building site has been sitting there for months with no progress."

"You're right, but my guy at Building and Planning seems to think all of Meadows's problems can magically disappear once his wife gets elected."

"If Tiana knew that, or maybe how that was going to play out, it might be motive enough for Meadows."

"Maybe. I reached out to him today. I need to do a little probing."

"I might be able to help you with that. Lulu texted me today. She's okay. She's in hiding, and she wants to meet with me."

A sharp pain lanced the back of his neck. "Is that

a good idea? Have you forgotten what happened the last time you two had a meeting?"

"This is different. She's aware of the danger now, and she's in a secure location. I might be able to get her talking about Kent. I don't think there's any love lost between those two."

"Be careful. No meetings in vacant dog parks."

"I promise I'll be careful. I think I took some heat off myself with this latest blog. Nobody can feel threatened by a tribute to the victim. I think I proved the threats intimidated me into backing off. Nobody knows we're working together."

"Nobody on my end knows." Denver glanced around the room. He'd catch hell if they did. "Keep me posted, anyway, and we'll touch base later."

"You, too. Denver..."

A pulse throbbed in his throat. "Yeah?"

"Let's get justice for the girl in the lake."

He let out a breath. "You got it."

When he ended the call, he tapped the edge of the phone against his chin. He jumped when it buzzed again. Had she decided to tell him what she'd really wanted to tell him?

He glanced at the display, disappointment bursting his bubble. "Mr. Meadows, thanks for calling back."

"Call me Kent, please. What can I do for you, Detective?"

"I want to talk with you again, Kent—in person."

"I'm busy today."

"It needs to be today."

"Do you mind coming downtown? I'm going to be having a meeting at my building site here, and I can chat with you when I'm done."

A muscle ticked in Denver's jaw. *Perfect.* "I can be there. What time?"

"Let's make it seven o'clock."

"In the dark?"

"We just switched to daylight savings. It's not that dark at seven, and the construction site is lit up like a Christmas tree most of the time."

"I'll be there."

Denver didn't have any intention of meeting with Kent Meadows at a half-finished construction site downtown without telling someone first. He notified Marino and told Billy Crouch, just in case Marino didn't remember or care.

With downtown LA on the way home to the Marina, Denver decided to put in some extra time and get a bite to eat before his meeting. Could he break Meadows at the place that had the power to break Meadows?

At around ten minutes to seven, Denver drove right onto the construction site, spitting up sand and gravel with the back tires of his sedan. Other cars dotted the flat area next to a giant hole, cement pylons and steel beams crisscrossing the vast space. Definitely stalled.

He pulled into the same row as two Teslas, a Porsche Cayenne and a classic Corvette. If Kent couldn't get money out of these people, he needed a new plan.

Denver waited in his car and sucked down the rest of the soda he'd got with his burger and fries. His phone pinged, and he read a message from Ashlynn that her meeting with Lulu was on. His thumb hesitated over the keyboard on his phone. He didn't have to tell her to be careful. She already knew that. They could trust Lulu, and Lulu knew to be careful, too.

Instead of sending her a cautionary text, he gave her a thumbs-up emoji.

A few minutes later, a woman and two men emerged from the bowels of the construction site. The woman picked her way over the gravel and slid into the Corvette.

One of the guys gave Denver a hard look before claiming one of the Teslas, and the other man turned and waved at the gaping hole in the earth as he unlocked his Porsche.

Denver exited his vehicle before the others drove away, just so that they could get a good look at him in case he wound up with a bullet in the back of the head at the bottom of that pit. As he walked closer to the site, he saw a small gray building with the Meadows Construction logo plastered all over it. Now he saw what the other guy had been waving at. Kent Meadows stood framed in the doorway of the outbuilding, casual in a pair of slacks and a cashmere sweater, his arms crossed.

Lights did illuminate the construction site, and a little porch lamp cast a yellow glow over Meadows, making his silver hair glint. Denver raised his hand as he strode forward, avoiding the potholes and dips.

"Welcome to my folly." Meadows spread his arms wide.

Jerking his thumb over his shoulder, Denver asked, "Any luck with that bunch?"

"Not really." He shrugged his sweater-clad shoulders. "Office? There's light and coffee and maybe a few snacks left over from the last construction workers who were here."

"How old would those snacks be?"

"About six months old, but this stuff has enough preservatives in it to last until the project gets completed."

"When will that be?" Denver crossed the threshold of the office and knocked over a pile of folders on his way to take a seat. "Sorry about that."

"That's all right." He waved a hand. "Someone will clean this up at some point." Meadows's thin lips twisted. "Probably won't be me."

"Unless your wife gets elected mayor."

Meadows chuckled. "Is that what this is about, Detective? You found out what a bottomless pit this project is for me and how much I need saving?"

"Something like that."

"Shh." He put his finger to his lips. "Don't tell anyone, but my wife doesn't have a chance."

"Does she know that?"

He shook his head. "That campaign manager of

hers keeps blowing smoke up…you know, in her face, and she believes him."

"But you weren't always so resigned, were you? You thought Veronica had a chance, and you thought this project had a chance."

"Not really." Meadows steepled his fingers. "Do you really think I killed a young woman to keep her quiet about my failing project? She wouldn't know about that, anyway. Meadows Plaza is not part of Veronica's campaign strategy, and that young woman was working for the campaign. I'd never met her. I don't involve myself with my wife's campaigns, except to foot the bills."

"You're sure you never met Tiana when she was at your house with you when your wife wasn't home?"

Meadows's face froze and the corner of his eye twitched. "Where did you hear that?"

"From a member of your household."

"Did that little snitch Lulu tell you?" He patted the side of his expensive haircut. "And after I set her up with a few of my friends, too."

"Set her up for what?"

"Exactly what she wanted, Detective. Look—" Meadows flattened his hands on the small dingy desk "—you don't have any proof that Tiana was at the house. I made sure any of our security footage showing her there was erased—and not because I murdered her but so that my wife wouldn't murder me. I had a fling with the girl. That's it. I was horrified when I learned of her death, but I wasn't involved. No motive."

"I can think of a few." Denver held up his hand and ticked off his fingers. "To keep your affair a secret. To keep her quiet about your plans for Meadows Plaza. Anger because she played you."

Meadows's head jerked up. "Played me? What do you mean?"

"Your wife didn't tell you? You haven't been following the news? Tiana Fuller was working for the Wexler campaign. She was a mole in your wife's campaign, looking for dirt. Seems that she found some."

Denver's words had sobered Meadows. His jaw tightened and his eyes narrowed. "That makes sense now. One day at the house, Tiana and I had drinks and I blacked out. I think she got into my computer that day."

"And discovered what?"

Meadows folded his hands, his knuckles white. "I'm not telling you any more, Detective Holt. You have no proof of anything and if Lulu told you about me and Tiana, she won't be able to testify to that."

Denver shot up in his chair, his fingertips buzzing. "Why is that? Did you kill her, too?"

"I didn't kill anyone, but we did send her away."

"Sent her away?" Denver's heart was pounding so hard, the buttons on his shirt were bouncing.

"After her stunt with that video, Veronica and I agreed it would be best if Lulu took a trip, so we sent her to Italy. She'd been wanting to go, anyway. She's sunning on the Italian Riviera about now, so she's not going to be telling tales about me."

Denver fumbled for his phone and jumped to his feet, sending the chair crashing behind him.

If Lulu was in Italy, who the hell was Ashlynn meeting tonight and why?

Chapter Twenty

Ashlynn crept along the path on the side of the Escalante mansion, the sparkling pool beyond the bushes to her right. She hadn't even seen the back quarters when she'd been here before. Then the path dipped to a clearing and a cozy house that merged with the canyon around it appeared like a cottage in a fairy tale. No wonder Lulu put up with her sister and the campaign. She had a sweet spot here.

Ashlynn knocked on the door, calling out, "Lulu? It's Ashlynn."

The door swung open and the other sister greeted her. "Hello, Ashlynn. Lulu had to go out, but when she told me she'd been expecting you, I thought we could meet instead. *LA Confidential* is a powerful force in the city, and I'd like to do a sit-down with you and discuss Tiana's role in the campaigns. Would you want to include a post like that? An exclusive with me?"

Ashlynn blinked. What a coup. "Of course I would, Councilwoman Escalante. Right now?"

"Sure, I'm actually free for a change." She gave

a little laugh. "Call me Veronica. It's a nice night. Let's sit by the pool."

"Will Lulu be joining us later? Is she okay? Did she tell you about being followed?"

"Lulu is safe now. She'll be by later. She did mention that she'd been followed and the two of you had been accosted. I can't believe the Wexler campaign would go to those lengths." She rolled her shoulders. "Amazing what some people will do for power."

Ashlynn started to turn to take the path back to the patio of the main house, and Veronica touched her arm. "Can I have your phone, Ashlynn? I don't want this recorded, at least not now. You can take notes, if you like."

Ashlynn patted her purse. "Okay. I understand. I won't record."

"I'd feel better if you left the phone here." Veronica shook a finger at her. "I know how you journalists are, so I have to insist just for my peace of mind."

"I suppose." She slipped her phone from her purse and handed it to Veronica.

Veronica tapped the case with a long fingernail. "I'll leave this in the cottage for safekeeping. Lulu and my mother also keep a fully stocked kitchen and bar. Can I get you something to drink?"

"Nothing alcoholic. I still have to maneuver my way down Mulholland."

"Such a pain, isn't it? We pay a price for living in the hills. I'll get us a couple of sodas."

Ashlynn traipsed back to the pool area, her step light. She'd come here just to touch base with Lulu, and she'd leave with an exclusive interview with a candidate for mayor.

As she sat on one of the lounge chairs, she dug in her purse for some paper and a pen. Was Veronica afraid she'd say something that could be used against her in the campaign and that she'd splash it over the blog? Ashlynn wasn't interested in the campaign, only as it related to Tiana's death.

As she settled a piece of paper on her knee, Veronica emerged from the path carrying two glasses in her hands. "Found some soda in the fridge. Will this do?"

"Thank you." Ashlynn took the drink from her and downed a few gulps before placing the glass on the little teak table between them. "What do you know about Tiana's spying on your behalf, and did you realize that she was a mole for the CREW?"

Veronica's generous lips tightened and her nostrils flared. "Jumping right in, aren't you?"

She'd agreed not to record the interview, but if Veronica expected softballs, she'd contacted the wrong blogger. Would anyone ever try to put one over on Sean?

She tapped the paper with her pen. "I'm sorry, Veronica. I'm not interested in how you got your start in politics or why you think you'd be better than Wexler for the city. *LA Confidential* is a true crime blog, and my readers and I are investigating the murder of a young woman who was involved in your campaign and in Mayor Wexler's. I want to know what she discovered."

Veronica raised her glass to Ashlynn. "Cheers to strong women getting down to business."

Ashlynn grabbed her glass and clinked it with Veronica's. "Cheers to strong women answering tough questions."

Veronica took a tiny sip of her drink and then ran her thumb up and down the condensation on the outside. "I didn't even know Tiana Fuller was working as a volunteer for our campaign...until she started having an affair with my husband."

Ashlynn sucked in a breath and took another gulp of her drink. "You knew about that?"

"I knew about all of Kent's affairs. I had a spy of my own—my mother. She kept an eye on things."

"Y-you didn't care?" Ashlynn rubbed her eye as the lights over the pool blurred.

"Look at this house. Look at my clothes, my car, my vacations." She snorted delicately. "Not bad for a girl from the barrio. I use Kent, and he does what he wants."

"That doesn't sound like a very good recipe for a marriage."

"It works. What would you know about it? Rich girl from San Marino."

Ashlynn swallowed against her dry throat. She took another sip of her drink, cupping the ice cube on her tongue. "I didn't realize you knew anything about me."

"When we found out Lulu had given you that video, Jed and I did a little investigating of our own—mostly Jed. Anyway—" she flicked her fingers "—the arrangement worked for me and Kent, or it had worked until Tiana Fuller showed up."

Ashlynn's heart thudded in her chest as her brain struggled to make sense of Veronica's words. This was important. This meant something. "Tiana? Why was she different?"

"Feeling okay?" Veronica leaned forward and stroked Ashlynn's hand, which could barely grip the pen. "Tiana became different the day I realized she'd gotten into Kent's computer—the idiot."

"Wh-what'd she find on Kent's…?" The pen dropped from Ashlynn's fingers and rolled off the table. She watched it dumbly, without reacting.

"She probably discovered that I'd been facilitating Kent's projects in the city for years—dummy corporations, money from phony sources, votes cast to grease the wheels of Kent's moneymaking machine." She clicked her tongue. "If any of that stuff ever came out, not only would I lose the mayor's race, I'd probably be heading to federal prison. I'm not doing that."

Ashlynn should probably feel more excitement, more horror at Veronica's pronouncements, but she felt only fatigue. She opened her mouth and tried to move her thick tongue. "You…you…"

"Well, not me personally." Veronica placed a hand over her heart. "I hired a couple of professionals to take care of the matter."

"Jed? K—?" Ashlynn couldn't remember the name of Veronica's husband. Blackness hovered on the periphery of her vision. This woman had drugged her.

Veronica tossed back her thick mane of brown hair. "Neither Jed nor Kent was involved, although I think Jed suspects something. Strong women—right, Ashlynn? I don't need a man to make power moves."

"Murder." Ashlynn screamed at her muscles to move, but all she could manage was to lift one finger.

"Murder is the biggest power move of all, and I'm done with this interview. On the bright side, just think of all the hits your blog's going to get when you go missing or when some hikers discover your body in six months or a year. You'll put *LA Confidential* on the national map."

DENVER LOOMED OVER Kent's desk, and the older man reached for the top drawer. Denver lunged toward him, slamming the drawer on his fingers. Kent wailed, clutching his bloody hand to his chest, the gun in the drawer forgotten. Denver grabbed the gun and pocketed it.

"Where is she? Where's your wife?"

Meadows gasped. "She wouldn't. She couldn't."

"Liar. You know what she's capable of." Denver shoved Meadows's phone into his chest. "Call her. Text her. And I'll be watching and listening, so don't tip her off."

"My wife did nothing." Meadows wiped his injured hand on the sleeve of his expensive sweater. "I'm not going to find her for you."

Denver slid his gun from his holster and leveled it at Meadows's head. "You're going to get on your phone right now, or I'm going to splatter your brains all over the plans for Meadows Plaza. You got me?"

"Y-you can't do this. I don't have a weapon. I'll sue you."

"You can't do that if you're dead." Denver smacked the phone on the table in the blood, and drops of it went airborne.

Meadows peered at him and then grabbed his phone. He entered the pass code with a misshapen finger and tapped the screen.

Denver growled. "Speaker."

The call rolled right to voice mail and a robotic voice answered.

"Text her."

Denver peered over Meadows's shoulder, the gun still aimed in Meadows's direction, as Meadows typed out a message to his wife, asking her where-abouts. The message hung there, undelivered.

Meadows coughed, cradling his hand. "She must have it turned off."

"Because she's committing a crime." Denver snatched up the phone before it could go into lock mode and scrolled through the apps until he found the one he wanted. "I knew you'd be tracking your wife's phone. Wouldn't want her surprising you with one of your sidepieces, right? Of course, she knew Tiana, figured out that she'd gotten some dirt on you—enough to sink you both."

Denver dashed the sweat from his eyes and squinted at the phone's display. He recognized the last location before she'd turned off her phone as her home in the hills above Sherman Oaks.

"Who's at the house now? Where's your mother-in-law? Do you have live-in staff?"

"I…"

Denver circled in front of Meadows, repositioning his gun to his Meadows's forehead, right between his eyes. "Not fast enough."

"We don't have live-in staff. My mother-in-law is in Mexico. We sent her there yesterday." Meadows choked. "Veronica's home alone. She'd do it there."

Denver pocketed Meadows's phone and hand-cuffed him to the desk so he couldn't warn his wife. He may have just ruined his chances with Homicide, but nothing mattered now but getting to Ashlynn.

As his car screamed from the construction site, he placed a call to the LAPD watch command. He ordered a unit to Escalante's address, claiming an assault in progress. At least, he prayed whatever was happening there was still in progress and not a done deal.

He turned on his blue and red revolvers and left the twinkling lights of downtown behind him as he sped down the 101, his adrenaline pumping through his system, his hands clenching the steering wheel.

Twenty minutes later as he careened off the free-way and hit Coldwater Canyon Boulevard, his phone rang and he flexed his fingers on the steering wheel. In his anxiety, he barked out, "What did you find?"

The sergeant on the other line said, "That's Coun-cilwoman Escalante's house."

"I know that. What did you find?"

"Nothing. Nobody's home."

"Send them back."

"Detective, this isn't the Northeast Division, and we have no cause to barge into the empty house of a member of the LA city council. Don't know about you, but I value my pension."

Denver cut him off and stomped on the accelerator, his tires squealing as he took a sharp curve. If he had to save Ashlynn himself, he would.

He cut his lights and cruised to a stop in front of the Escalante mansion. Lights embedded in the flower garden lit the front of the house and guided him to the double doors. The cops had probably already rung the doorbell. They didn't get an answer, and he didn't expect one, either.

He slid his weapon from its holster. He crept around the side of the house and spotted a side gate standing open.

He sidled through the space sideways, not trusting that the hinges on the gate would stay silent. He avoided the flagstones, and his shoes squished against the dirt and grass. As he peered around the corner of the house onto the patio, his heart stuttered in his chest.

LA City Councilwoman Veronica Escalante knelt by the side of the pool, both hands in the water, pushing something beneath the surface. Had Ashlynn given up the fight? Had Escalante already killed her?

Denver charged forward, leaping over a chaise longue, his gun aloft. "Stop what you're doing! Stop!"

With her arms in the water up to her elbows, Veronica cranked her head to the side and her mouth
dropped open. "I—I'm trying to save her. She fell in."

"Get away from the pool, and put your hands up
where I can see them."

"I'm Councilwoman Escalante. This woman tried
to drown herself in my pool." She sat back on her
heels, her arms hanging by her sides, dripping water.

Oh, God. Was Ashlynn dead already?

Denver ran to the side of the pool, knocking Veronica backward. Ashlynn was floating on her stomach, her arms splayed to the sides, her hair creating a
red fan in the water. He shoved his gun in his waistband and reached to pull her toward the edge.

Grabbing handfuls of her clothing, he rolled her
from the pool and onto her back. He pumped her
chest and listened for her breath. "C'mon. C'mon,
Ashlynn."

He applied another compression and she coughed
up water, her eyelids fluttering. "That's my girl."

"Sh-she drugged me." Her eyes opened and then
widened at the same time he felt Veronica snatch
his gun.

He spun around, staring down the barrel of his
own weapon.

Veronica's hand trembled. "I told you I tried to
save her. She's one of my husband's lovers, a volunteer. When Kent broke things off with her, she came
here to kill herself."

"Did you kill Tiana Fuller yourself, or did you hire
someone?" Smiling slowly, he nodded at her shaky

grip on the gun. "You farmed that one out, just like you hired someone to intimidate your own sister and Ashlynn at the dog park that night. You don't even know how to hold a weapon properly. It's a lot different from drugging someone and holding her head under water, isn't it?"

"I—I told you what happened."

"I know exactly what happened. You didn't care that your husband was seeing Tiana until you discovered she'd stumbled onto your little personal money train where you were funneling funds into Kent's shell companies."

Her dark eyes smoldered. "You're crazy. You came barging in here, demanding answers from me, demanding answers from Ashlynn Hughes from *LA Confidential*. When you didn't get what you wanted, you shot Ashlynn. While you were pushing her into the pool, I got your gun and shot you."

"That's a lot of setup to manage, Councilwoman, especially as it's clear you know nothing about guns and Ashlynn will have drugs in her system. How are you going to explain that?" He inched closer to her, still in a crouched position, sliding his hand up his pant leg and curling his fingers around the handle of his knife.

"Just because she's a blogger doesn't mean she wasn't having an affair with my husband. I'll stick to my original story. She came here to kill herself. I was reasoning with her until you crashed the party, desperate to solve this case, desperate to wrest it back from the blogger. It's no secret that the LAPD hates *LA Confidential.* I can pull it off." She tossed her head. "Do you know who I am?"

He lunged toward her, yanking the knife from its sheath around his leg. As she stumbled back, firing wildly into the air, he swung the blade, making contact with her side.

She screamed and dropped the gun, clutching her wound as it gushed blood.

He kicked the gun out of her reach and twisted around toward Ashlynn, her chest rising and falling, despite the paralysis of the rest of her body. He pulled her into his lap. "You're going to be okay. Everything's going to be okay."

Then he grabbed his phone and pointed it at Veronica, writhing on the patio, blood oozing between her fingers. "I know exactly who you are. You're the suspect under arrest for the murder of Tiana Fuller."

Epilogue

A few days later, Ashlynn answered her door and pulled Denver into her place. "How'd it go?"

"When Veronica saw the evidence we had against her—Kent's computer, her prints on my gun, your testimony against her, the drugs she used on you in the guest cottage—she confessed from her hospital bed. She gave up the two hitmen who killed Tiana, too. If she's going down, she's bringing everyone with her."

"I had no doubt you'd nail her either with the evidence or a confession, but I meant how'd that other thing go?" She held on to his hands, lacing her fingers through his.

"Suspended." He lifted his broad shoulders that had carried so much.

She squeezed his hands. He'd given up his career aspirations to save her. "I'm sorry, Denver. Even though you solved this case, does that mean they're not going to bring you on to Homicide?"

"I wouldn't say that." He raised her hands to his lips and kissed her fingers. "I could use a beer."

She disentangled herself and scooted past him into the kitchen. "So, there's still hope for you?"

"Let's put it this way. Billy Crouch and Jake McAllister, the two superstars of Robbery-Homicide, took me aside today, congratulated me on the case, and said, if anything, the way I questioned Meadows to get to his wife was a bright golden star next to my name, as far as they were concerned."

"Is Meadows going to sue the department?" She dipped into her fridge to grab two bottles of beer.

As he took a bottle from her, he snorted. "He can try…from federal prison. I think he's going to be busy with his high-priced attorneys for a while."

She grabbed his hand again and led him to the couch. "Poor Tiana. She craved the excitement of a political campaign and got in over her head. She never slept with Kent, you know. It was all a big tease to get into the house. Lulu told me that."

"I think Tiana watched too many TV shows. She had this unrealistic view, and didn't realize how far people would go to protect their interests."

"One thing that's been bothering me is how did she wind up in a Wexler vehicle? Did Veronica order her thugs to steal a Wexler car to frame the mayor?"

He combed his fingers through her hair. "That just fell into their laps. Tiana already had that car. She'd taken it herself and used it for her covert operations. She drove out in the car to meet who she thought was someone from the Wexler campaign. She was ambushed by the hitmen, dumped in the trunk, and pushed into the lake."

"Convenient for Veronica, but also a mistake. In the end, if Tiana hadn't been in a CREW car, she never would've been connected to either campaign. Neither campaign would've claimed her, and Tony would've been too afraid to step forward. Maybe Lulu would've come through."

"How is Lulu?" Denver rubbed a circle on her back. "At least she tried to do the right thing, regardless of her motives."

"She's fine. She's still in Italy. She wasn't that surprised about the turn of events. She always knew her sister was ruthless, even though Lulu was supposedly the black sheep of the family."

"Is that why you two connected?" Denver tapped the neck of his bottle against hers.

"Maybe." Ashlynn scraped a nail through the foil label on her damp bottle. "What did you think of the blog?"

She hated asking, but it still mattered to her. She'd proved that by stumbling into a dangerous situation with Veronica just to get an exclusive.

"It was great. Your writing is top-notch, but is that you? Scrabbling for a story almost got you killed—several times."

Turning toward him, she traced a fingertip along his jaw. "It also brought you into my life."

He captured her finger and sucked it into his mouth. "As much as I get a thrill out of rescuing you, I want to make sure I stay in your life and you stay in mine. You're sure you don't want to go back to writing about fashion?"

"But we did it, didn't we? We did it together."

He wiggled his eyebrows. "We've done several things together. Which one do you mean?"

"Justice for the girl in the lake." She held out her fist for a bump. "Justice for Tiana."

He tapped her fist with his and then pulled her into his arms to kiss her long and hard. When he released her, he put a finger against her lower lip. "Does that mean fashion is out and true crime stays?"

"I'm ending the blog and starting a podcast." She curled a leg beneath her and cupped his face with both hands. "It's going to be all mine, something Sean never did. I'm going to put my own spin on it, my own stamp."

He encircled her wrists with his fingers. "You're going to need a contact, someone on the inside, someone not afraid to break a few rules. You're going to need me."

And then he showed her just how much she did need him.

* * * * *

Look for more books in Carol Ericson's
The Lost Girls series coming in 2023.
And be sure to look for the first title,
Canyon Crime Scene, *available now*
wherever Harlequin Intrigue books are sold!

COMING NEXT MONTH FROM

(H) HARLEQUIN

INTRIGUE

#2091 MISSING WITNESS AT WHISKEY GULCH
The Outriders Series • by Elle James

Shattering loss taught former Delta Force operative Becker Jackson to play things safe. Still, he can't turn down Olivia Swann's desperate plea to find her abducted sister—nor resist their instant heat. But with two mob families targeting them, can they save an innocent witness—and their own lives—in time?

#2092 LOOKS THAT KILL
A Procedural Crime Story • by Amanda Stevens

Private investigator Natalie Bolt has secrets—and not just about the attempted murder she witnessed. But revealing her true identity to prosecutor Max Winter could cost her information she desperately needs. Max has no idea their investigation will lead to Natalie herself. Or that the criminals are still targeting the woman he's falling for...

#2093 LONE WOLF BOUNTY HUNTER
STEALTH: Shadow Team • by Danica Winters

Though he prefers working solo, bondsman Trent Lockwood teams up with STEALTH attorney Kendra Spade to hunt down a criminal determined to ruin both their families. The former cowboy and the take-charge New Yorker may share a common enemy, but the stakes are too high to let their attraction get in the way...

#2094 THE BIG ISLAND KILLER
Hawaii CI • by R. Barri Flowers

Detective Logan Ryder is running out of time to stop a serial killer from claiming a fourth woman on Hawaii's Big Island. Grief counselor Elena Kekona puts her life on the line to help when she discovers he resembles the victims. But Elena's secrets could result in a devastating endgame that both might not survive...

#2095 GUNSMOKE IN THE GRASSLAND
Kings of Coyote Creek • by Carla Cassidy

Deputy Jacob Black has his first assignment: solve the murder of Big John King. Ashley King is surprised to learn her childhood crush is working to find her father's killer. But when Ashley narrowly fends off a brutal attack, Jacob's new mission is to keep her safe—and find the killer at any cost.

#2096 COLD CASE SUSPECT
by Kayla Perrin

After fleeing Sheridan Falls to escape her past, Shayla Phillips is back in town to join forces with Tavis Saunders—whose cousin was a victim of a past crime. The former cop won't rest until he solves the case. But can they uncover the truth before more lives are lost?

YOU CAN FIND MORE INFORMATION ON UPCOMING HARLEQUIN TITLES, FREE EXCERPTS AND MORE AT HARLEQUIN.COM.

HICNM0722

Don't miss the next book in

B.J. DANIELS

Buckhorn, Montana series

Order your copy today!

HQNBooks.com

SPECIAL EXCERPT FROM

H HARLEQUIN

INTRIGUE

*The Big Island Killer is terrorizing the women of Hawaii
and it's up to Detective Logan Ryder and his task force
to find and capture this elusive criminal. Then he meets
and falls for Elena Kekona, who matches the victims'
profile, and suddenly the case becomes very personal...*

Keep reading for a sneak peek at
The Big Island Killer,
the first book in R. Barri Flowers's Hawaii CI series.

"How did you end up on the Big Island?"

"To make a long story short, I was recruited by the Hawaii
Police Department to fill an opening, after working with the
California Department of Justice's Human Trafficking and
Sexual Predator Apprehension Team. Guess I had become
burned out at that point in investigating trafficking cases, often
involving the sexual exploitation of women and children, and
decided I needed to move in a different direction."

Elena took another sip of her drink. "Any regrets?"

Reading her mind, Logan supposed she wondered if going
after human traffickers and sexual predators in favor of serial
killers and other homicide-related offenders was much of a
trade-off. He saw both as equally heinous in nature, but the
incidence was much greater with the former than the latter.
Rather than delve too deeply into those dynamics, instead he
told her earnestly, while appreciating the view across the table,
"From where I'm sitting at this moment, I'd have to say no
regrets whatsoever."

She blushed and uttered, "You're smooth in skillfully dodging the question, I'll give you that."

He grinned, enjoying this easygoing communication between them. Where else could it lead? "On balance, having the opportunity to live and work in Hawaii, even if it's less than utopia, I'd gladly do it over again."

"I'm glad you made that choice, Logan," Elena said sincerely, meeting his eyes.

"So am I." In that moment, it seemed like an ideal time to kiss her—those soft lips that seemed ever inviting. Leaning his face toward her, Logan watched for a reaction that told him they weren't on the same wavelength. Seeing no indication otherwise, he went in for the kiss. It was everything he expected—sweet, sensual and intoxicating. Only when his cell phone chimed did he grudgingly pull away. He removed the phone from his pocket, glanced at the caller ID and told Elena, "I need to get this."

"Please do," she said understandingly.

Before he even put the phone to his ear, Logan sensed that he would not like what he heard. He listened anyway as Ivy spoke in a near frantic tone. Afterward, he hung up and looked gloomily at Elena, and said, "The body of a young woman has been found." He paused, almost hating to say this, considering the concerns he still had for the safety of the grief counselor and not wanting to unnerve her. But there was no denying the truth or sparing her what she needed to hear. "It appears that the Big Island Killer has struck again."

Don't miss
The Big Island Killer *by R. Barri Flowers,*
available September 2022 wherever
Harlequin Intrigue books and ebooks are sold.

Harlequin.com

HIEXP0722

Love Harlequin romance?

DISCOVER.
Be the first to find out about promotions,
news and exclusive content!

Facebook.com/HarlequinBooks

Twitter.com/HarlequinBooks

Instagram.com/HarlequinBooks

Pinterest.com/HarlequinBooks

YouTube.com/HarlequinBooks

ReaderService.com

EXPLORE.
Sign up for the Harlequin e-newsletter and
download a free book from any series at
TryHarlequin.com

CONNECT.
Join our Harlequin community to
share your thoughts and connect
with other romance readers!
Facebook.com/groups/HarlequinConnection

HSOCIAL2021